ARE YOU AT RISK FOR PUBLIC SHAMING?

ARE YOU AT RISK FOR PUBLIC SHAMING?

Sherri Mabry Gordon

GOT ISSUES?

E Enslow Publishing
101 W. 23rd Street
Suite 240
New York, NY 10011
USA
enslow.com

Published in 2016 by Enslow Publishing, LLC
101 W. 23rd Street, Suite 240, New York, NY 10011

Library of Congress Cataloging-in-Publication Data
Names: Gordon, Sherri Mabry.
Title: Are you at risk for public shaming? / Sherri Mabry Gordon.
Description: New York : Enslow Publishing, 2016. | Series: Got Issues? | Includes index.
Identifiers: ISBN 978-0-7660-7136-0
Subjects: LCSH: Shame—Juvenile literature. | Interpersonal relations—Juvenile literature. | Shame—Social aspects.
Classification: LCC BF575.S45 G67 2016 | DDC 152.4—dc23

Printed in the United States of America

To Our Readers: We have done our best to make sure all websites in this book were active and appropriate when we went to press. However, the author and the publisher have no control over and assume no liability for the material available on those websites or on any websites they may link to. Any comments or suggestions can be sent by e-mail to customerservice@enslow.com.

Disclaimer: For many of the images in this book, the people photographed are models. The depictions do not imply actual situations or events.

Photo Credits: Cover, p. 3 PathDoc/Shutterstock.com (girl with cell phone); p. 6 pockygallery/Shutterstock.com; p. 7 Marc Piasecki/Getty Images Entertainment/Getty Images; p. 9 © North Wind Picture Archives; p. 11 antoniodiaz/Shutterstock.com; pp. 14, 49 © AP Images; p. 15 SpeedKingz/Shutterstock.com; p. 17 ArtFamily/Shutterstock.com; p. 19 oliveromg/Shutterstock.com; p. 22 Photographee.eu/Shutterstock.com; p. 26 Nico Traut/Shutterstock.com; p. 28 Daniel Grill/Getty Images; p. 31 MLADEN ANTONOV/AFP/Getty Images; p. 35 EMMANUEL DUNAND/AFP/Getty Images; p. 36 Eduardo Cervantes/Shutterstock.com; p. 39 © AP Images; p. 42 KatarzynaBialasiewicz/iStock/Thinkstock; p. 44 Deymos.HR/Shutterstock.com; p. 47 iStock.com/icafreitas; p. 51 wrangler/Shutterstock.com; p. 53 Stockbyte/Thinkstock; p. 56 fstop123/E+/Getty Images; p. 57 Haslam Photography/Shutterstock.com; p. 60 Bloomua/Shutterstock.com; p. 62 GWImages/Shutterstock.com; p. 64 iStock.com/Darkcloud; pp. 67, 83 Monkey Business Images/Shutterstock.com; p. 71 C Flanigan/WireImage/Getty Images; p. 73 Golden Pixels LLC/Shutterstock.com; p. 75 iStock.com/digitalskillet; p. 77 iStock.com/Leontura; p. 81 iStock.com/ClarkandCompany; p. 87 sirawit hengthabthim/Shutterstock.com; p. 88 iStock.com/yuoak; p. 89 Samuel Borges Photography/Shutterstock.com.

Contents

SCANDAL

1 Public Shaming Then and Now

"At the age of 22, I fell in love with my boss. At the age of 24, I learned the devastating consequences," says Monica Lewinsky in the first few minutes of her TED Talk about public shaming.

"Like me . . . a few of you may also have taken wrong turns by falling in love with the wrong person. Maybe even your boss," she continues. "Unlike me, though, your boss probably wasn't the president of the United States of America . . . Not a day goes by that I'm not reminded of my mistake, and I regret that mistake deeply."[1]

In 1998, Lewinsky, who had been an intern in the White House, became well known following a romantic relationship with married President Bill Clinton. She also is one of the first high-profile examples of how public shaming can take control of a person's identity and shred it.

Monica Lewinsky has spoken to the media and presented a TED talk on public shaming. The former White House intern was shamed and ostracized for having an affair with President Bill Clinton.

"This scandal was brought to you by the digital revolution," she explains. "That meant we could access all the information we wanted, when we wanted it, anytime, anywhere, and when the story broke . . . it broke online. It was the first time the traditional news was usurped by the Internet for a major news story. [It was] a click that reverberated around the world."[2]

Nearly overnight, Lewinsky went from being a private figure to a publicly shamed one. "I was patient zero of losing a personal reputation on a global scale almost instantaneously," she says.

"This rush to judgment, enabled by technology, led to mobs of virtual stone-throwers," Lewinsky explains. "Granted, it was before social media, but people could still comment online, email stories, and, of course, email cruel jokes."[3]

What's more, she was on the cover of every major newspaper and the butt of every late-night joke. She also was branded everything from a tart, a tramp, and a slut to a whore and a bimbo. It turned her life upside down. At one point, she even contemplated suicide.

Today, public shaming like what Lewinsky experienced is becoming "a blood sport that has to stop," she says. "Now that social media has been born, the landscape has sadly become much more populated with [public shaming] instances."[4]

While shaming, bullying, and cruelty to others is not a new concept, this mean behavior reaches more people online now than ever before. And it never goes away. Now instead of just a community shaming another person for something he or she did wrong, a virtual community comprised of millions of people can share in the shaming of another person—often anonymously. It is always out there for people to read.

"There are no perimeters around how many people can publicly observe you and put you in a public stockade," Lewinsky says. "There is a very personal price to public humiliation, and the growth of the Internet has jacked up that price."[5]

Public Shaming Throughout History

Publicly shaming someone is not a new concept. In fact, it is one of the oldest ways to punish society's offenders. Centuries ago, villagers would cast out those they considered dishonored. In Colonial America, they used stockades to publicly shame people. Flogging, branding, and pillories also were used to shame people.

In the United States, public shaming was slowly phased out around the 1900s. However, some states kept public shaming practices in place for years. For example, Delaware kept the pillory until 1905 and public whippings until 1972.[6]

During America's colonial period, public shaming took a slightly different form than it does today. Offenders were regularly humiliated by being locked into stockades in village squares.

Perhaps one of the best-known examples of public shaming was illustrated in the classic novel *The Scarlett Letter*, written by Nathaniel Hawthorne in 1850. Set in 1642 in the Puritan town of Boston, the book begins with a crowd gathering to witness the punishment of Hester Prynne, a young woman found guilty of adultery. To shame her for her actions, she was required to wear a scarlet letter A, which stood for adulterer. She stood on the scaffold for three hours and was exposed to public humiliation.

When people lived in small close-knit communities where people knew each other, like the one described in Hawthorne's book, this public display of punishment was humiliating and meant to degrade someone for doing something society felt was wrong. The goal was to keep the offender from making the same mistake again.

Today, people are not just rebuked like in years past. Social media tools such as Facebook, Twitter, YouTube, and Instagram are the new town squares, and the audience is much more vast. The people passing judgment often do not even live in the same community, and many times they do not even know each other.

With the simple click of a button, they can play judge and jury and condemn someone they do not even know. The end result is often the complete destruction of a person's life. The images and words often haunt the person for years afterward.

Public Shaming Today

According to experts, public shaming is a natural human urge. People feel the need to point out what others are doing wrong and often believe by shaming them they can change the behavior. The Internet has become the perfect vehicle to highlight another person's missteps and mistakes.

What's more, some experts speculate that people who publicly shame others have an incentive to do so. They gain popularity in the digital community and increase their base of online followers. For many, this is all the motivation they need to attack another person.[7]

Today, public shaming can take place in the online world. Through social media, we can be judged mercilessly by people we do not even know, for things we may or may not have done.

"This desire we have to be like amateur detectives, [looking for] clues of people's inherent evil by finding the worst tweet they ever wrote, is not only wrong; it's damaging," says Jon Ronson, author of *So You Have Been Publicly Shamed*. What starts out as disapproval ends up as "a complete shaming of the person."[8]

Publicly shaming someone is not limited by age, race, or socioeconomic status. Anyone can be publicly shamed. In fact, more than one in four American teens have witnessed cruel behavior on social networks. Eighty-nine percent say that behavior takes place on Facebook, according to a study by McAfee. That is a lot of kids, according to Marc Brackett, a researcher at the Yale Center for Emotional Intelligence, who helped facilitate the study. Ninety-three percent of all American teens have Facebook accounts, he says.[9]

"Teens take a lot of risks," Brackett says. "They're concerned with their reputation, and they're hijacked by emotions. Peer relationships are a critical focus for them." In a thirty-day experiment on the site, Brackett and Robin Stern, also with the Yale Center for Emotional Intelligence, found that in the range of emotions the young adults felt, anger and embarrassment dominated. When you combine teen impulsiveness with such strong emotions, you have the perfect recipe for public shaming.[10]

The Flip Side of Public Shaming

There are times when there are positive uses for Internet shaming, says Ronson. For instance, he points to Twitter hashtags, such as #BlackLivesMatter, #WhyIStayed, and #YesAllWomen. Hashtags such as these are useful in highlighting social issues that were once hidden.

Take the hashtag #WhyIStayed as an example. This hashtag became popular after the video of Ray Rice hitting his wife Janay went viral. Ray Rice was a professional football player with the Baltimore Ravens. The video had people on Twitter questioning why she stayed with him. Survivors of domestic violence began

Practice Digital Etiquette

One way to avoid public shaming is to make sure you have strong digital etiquette skills. Here are five things you need to remember about online communication.

Treat others the way you want to be treated. In other words, you need to have good manners, even online. Be kind to others, and avoid making mean or snide comments. Also, make it a habit not to discuss personal or volatile issues online. Instead, have these discussions in person. Never post something mean online—no matter how angry or upset you are.

Make sure your posts are positive and truthful. You should never post rumors or gossip. Even liking or commenting on a post that attacks another person's reputation is not a good idea. Also avoid making jokes or engaging in sarcasm. These usually fall flat online because all people can see are the words. They cannot hear your voice or see your face to know you are joking.

Stop and think before you hit send or post. Once you press send, there is no way to take back your words. When you are online, make it a habit to read and reread your comments and posts before clicking. One mistake can hurt you or another person.

Do not share another person's story. If it is not your story to tell, you should not be telling it. Likewise, you should not post pictures, videos, or screenshots of other people without their permission. Think about how you would feel if someone shared an embarrassing photo or video of you.

Avoid the drama. Learn how to exit a conversation that is taking a wrong turn, especially if it is getting mean or rude. Do not respond, comment, like, or post to conversations that are not kind and positive. No good will come from posting a nasty response or making a negative comment.[11]

tweeting their own stories of why they stayed and added the hashtag #WhyIStayed.

Tweets included things such as, "I tried to leave the house once after an abusive episode, and he blocked me. He slept in front of the door that entire night. #WhyIStayed," or "Because every time was the last time. #WhyIStayed."[12]

The goal was to change the conversation about domestic violence. Advocates wanted people to realize that leaving is not as easy as it sounds. And instead of asking, "Why doesn't she leave?" or shaming her because she stayed with him, they should be asking, "Why does he hit her?"[13]

Janay and Ray Rice made the news when security footage showing Ray abusing Janay leaked to the public. Both parties endured public shaming for their roles in and reactions to the incident.

Cyberbullying is a growing and dangerous offshoot of public shaming. With just a few anonymous clicks, one person can intimidate another, without breaking a sweat.

"Shaming can be really, really powerful," Ronson says. The question is, can people learn to use it for more than vindication and personal entertainment?[14]

It Is All a Matter of Perspective

According to Lewinsky, preventing public shaming is all about context. "What's happened with the Internet is that we lose context for a story, but we [also] lose context for a person," she says. "This is someone's daughter. This is someone's sister. This is somebody that has a sense of humor that might be different from mine. This is someone who has a long range of life experiences, which inform how they themselves, view the world, or how they articulate themselves."[15]

She suggests imagining what it would be like to walk a mile in someone else's shoes and to think before you click. "With every click, we make a choice," she says. "The more we saturate our culture with public shaming, the more accepted it is, the more we will see behavior like cyberbullying, trolling, some forms of hacking, and online harassment."[16]

Stephen Marche, a columnist for *Esquire* and author of five books, agrees. He suggests that people learn a new way to communicate that allows them to overcome the "facelessness" of the Internet. He suggests that people remember that behind every tweet, text, or post, there are real people. These faceless people have hopes, dreams, families, and so much more. As a result, they should not be defined by one poorly worded tweet, text, post, or action. "We need a new art of conversation for the new conversations we are having," he says.[17]

2

An Inside Look at Public Shaming

Integrity is something Jean-Marc had always valued. So when a public shaming incident put his integrity in question, he began struggling to accept what was happening. His marriage was crumbling. His integrity as the youth soccer commissioner was in question. And most importantly, how he felt about himself was deteriorating.

"Integrity is important to me no matter what else. Before the incident, I felt that people knew that they could trust me," says Jean-Marc. "Now all these people that had looked at me for expertise and credibility were questioning my integrity. When everyone in the community knows that you did X, there is no way not to have that affect you."[1]

The catalyst for Jean-Marc's public shaming began when he had an Internet affair with a publicist involved in the soccer organization. They began exchanging romantic e-mails on a consistent basis until they had second thoughts and ended their affair. But a year and a half later, the woman's husband discovered the e-mails.

"All the wheels on the bus came off at that point," says Jean-Marc. "This was before social media, so he took advantage of chat rooms and community bulletin boards online to smear me all over the place. He also had access to the names and addresses of seven hundred sets of parents [in the youth soccer organization] and sent e-mails out to everyone. He said things like, 'This guy could potentially molest your kids,' and so on. Literally everyone in town knew what had happened, and many thought it was worse than it really was. It didn't matter that he wasn't being truthful."[2]

Overnight, Jean-Marc went from being the trusted youth soccer commissioner, Sunday school teacher, and community friend to someone people questioned and worried about. People in town looked at him differently, and some even treated him differently.

"He was every bit the angry—and justifiably so—husband," says Jean-Marc. "But not everything he was saying was factual . . . Anytime I would go to the grocery store or church [in our small town], I would run into someone involved in the soccer program. I would always be thinking, 'Does this person know?' and 'What kind of crap is he saying about me?'"[3]

The end result of the shaming was that Jean-Marc and his wife divorced. "She said she couldn't walk around town without people knowing her husband had cheated on her," he says.[4]

Eventually, he did confront the man shaming him.

"After being cowed by this guy for six months in a row, I finally said to him, 'Look, my marriage ended, and I feel bad showing myself in town. You have accomplished everything you wanted to accomplish. But I am not going to be cowed by you any longer.' By doing that, he started leaving me alone."[5]

While the shaming campaign did come to an end, the damage had already been done. Jean-Marc's marriage was over. He had lost some of his standing in the community, and he had to wonder all the time what people thought of him. About a year later, he accepted a position in another state. To this day, he still struggles when he returns to the town.

A message put out by just one person can have extremely serious consequences for another. Shaming campaigns have been conducted by people who insist that they are morally right.

"Shame is on you. It doesn't matter if anyone else says anything. You feel the embarrassment all the time," says Jean-Marc. "I accept responsibility for what I did. I don't try to get around it. I violated people's trust in me, and I violated my marriage vows. But the Internet is a very one-dimensional tool. There is so much more to a person than that one mistake."[6]

The Problem With Public Shaming Today

Today, public shaming is so much more than shaming a person for making morally wrong decisions through insensitive jokes and hateful comments. It has morphed into something immense and, at times, uncontrollable. Many experts believe the public shaming we see today is in essence mob justice. Mob justice occurs when authority is suddenly given to the masses, and they collectively decide the fate of the person being targeted.

As a result, there is a total disconnect between the severity of the crime and the punishment of the offender. And unlike public shaming of the past, where the community was small, the Internet has propelled shaming into dangerous territory. Now when someone is publicly shamed, the message gets out faster, is easier to send, and reaches more people than ever before. Anyone anywhere can join the online mob.[7]

The problem with this type of mob justice is that it can spiral out of control and far beyond what many shamers even imagined. As a result, public shaming can look more like a tool designed to satisfy the crowd rather than a method for punishing the wrongdoer. The anonymity that often comes with public shaming can lead to harsher consequences than are warranted. Many of these consequences are due to what experts refer to as schadenfreude.

Schadenfreude occurs when people get pleasure from the misfortune of others. Researchers indicate that when people experience schadenfreude, it can make them feel better about themselves. In other words, it is self-affirming.

"If somebody enjoys the misfortune of others, then there's something in that misfortune that is good for the person," says Wilco van Dijk, a researcher with Leiden University in the Netherlands who has studied schadenfreude. In other words, people who publicly shame others get something from the experience. For example, they might feel the person deserves what is happening, or they may have low self-esteem, and the public shaming makes them feel good about themselves.[8]

"I think when you have low self-esteem, you will do almost anything to feel better, and when you're confronted with the misfortune of others, you'll feel schadenfreude," says van Dijk. "What we found is [people] have less schadenfreude [when they are affirmed in some way]—they don't need the misfortune of others to feel better anymore."[9]

Van Dijk says that just about everyone experiences schadenfreude at some point in his or her life. "[However] . . . if you feel schadenfreude without any sympathy or compassion for that other person, that would not be good," van Dijk says. "Our society thrives on compassion and empathy."[10]

Consequently, it should come as no surprise that the antidote for public shaming is emotional intelligence. Emotional intelligence, or a person's EQ, is the ability to recognize emotions in other people and change reactions and behaviors accordingly.

Rosalind Wiseman, author of *Queen Bees and Wannabes,* says teens need to learn how to be socially competent in a complex world. She adds that while abuse of power is inevitable, teens need to learn that "people's dignity is not negotiable, for them or for anyone."[11]

Is Cyberbullying Just Another Name for Shaming?

When it comes to cyberbullying and public shaming, they both involve humiliating another person online. They also both involve online activities such as:

- Sharing embarrassing photos of the victim on social media or through another public forum
- Making threats or calling the victim names in social media posts
- Using texts, tweets, instant messages, and e-mails to send cruel or threatening messages
- Uploading a video that embarrasses the victim
- Creating a fake social media profile on Facebook, Twitter, or Instagram and pretending to be the victim
- Posting rumors or gossip about the victim

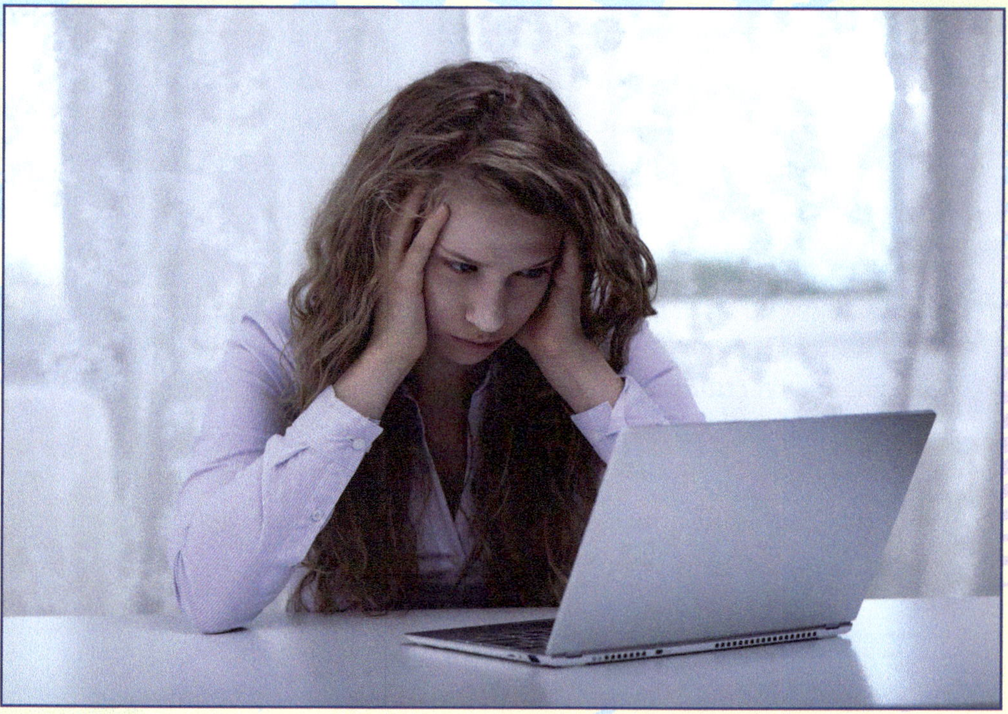

Cyberbullying is more "personal" than public shaming. The cyberbully knows the victim and the torment is carried out by a small group of people. Both forms of humiliation can make a person's life miserable.

- Developing a social media page meant exclusively for harassing the victim
- Sharing the victim's personal information
- Adding the victim's name to a public list online, such as smut lists or ugly lists

The difference is that public shaming is often considered acceptable by large groups of people, while most people feel cyberbullying is wrong and needs to be addressed and prevented. Additionally, with public shaming there is agreement among large groups of people that humiliating a person online is appropriate when someone has done something wrong. It is common for people to think that a perpetrator deserves to be demeaned.

Another difference between cyberbullying and public shaming is the scale to which others are involved. Usually, cyberbullying occurs when one or two people attack another person online. This initial attack may then lead to others to joining in, or it may just involve one or two people as the tormentors. But the group of people cyberbullying the victim is usually not as large as the group involved in a public shaming incident.

While it is true that sometimes cyberbullying will involve a large group of people, usually everyone knows the person being bullied. Occasionally, a stranger might contribute to the cyberbullying by adding a comment or two, but typically the cyberbullying is limited in scope compared to public shaming.

Meanwhile, public shaming occurs on a much broader scale, and many times it is perpetuated by complete strangers. What's more, public shaming incidents typically go viral with hundreds of thousands to millions of people viewing the incident, many of whom will make a comment or repost the incident.

In simpler terms, with cyberbullying the victim remains a private citizen. Meanwhile, with public shaming the public recognizes a publicly shamed victim. He or she goes from being a private citizen to a public one. Both victims experience shame, embarrassment, and humiliation, but the extent to which the world knows about it is much different.

How Does Public Shaming Happen?

According to experts, there are a variety of reasons why public shaming occurs. Aside from the easy access to information and the growing use of social media, there are a number of reasons why public shaming seems to be on the rise. What's more, the Internet has made it easier for people all around the world to connect. But with this growth has come an increase in narcissism, especially on social media.

As a result, people with high levels of narcissism are posting more frequently to social media and tagging themselves in photos.[12] This type of self-promotion can lead to public shaming. In other words, teens who spend a lot of time posting selfies and making random comments online increase their risk of being publicly shamed for it. Here are some additional reasons why public shaming occurs.

Context is blurred online. Another name for this phenomenon is context collapse, which is a term used by researchers to describe the effects of social media. In other words, online there is an infinite audience possible as opposed to the limited audience people typically have offline. In an offline audience, a person will adjust his or her tone, facial expressions, and presentation of self to fit the social context. On social media, this is not possible, so the context collapses. What's more, posts and comments that would normally be made to a smaller audience made up of people the poster knows will not be received the same way by the larger audience. For this reason, jokes online fall flat and sarcasm is missed.

Snap judgments are made. Because people cannot see a person's face or hear the person's tone of voice, a comment online is not taken in the same way that it would be taken offline. Additionally, social media does not provide context for what a person is saying. But people do not consider these facts. Instead, they take the words at face value and make snap judgments about people. Because they can instantly repost, retweet, forward, and share the comments, they encourage others to make the same snap judgments without context.

Distribution is instant and massive. In a matter of a few short minutes, a careless tweet, a poorly worded Facebook post, or an inappropriate photo on Instagram can be copied, shared, retweeted, and reposted. If enough people are intrigued or outraged by what they see or read, the message can go viral in what feels like an instant. Suddenly, the invisible public has turned into a massive invisible public.[13]

Types of Public Shaming

Most of the time public shaming occurs because of a poorly worded tweet, insensitive joke, racist remark, or other wrongdoing that the public wants to magnify on the Internet. Sometimes parents will shame kids online for making mistakes or breaking rules. Other times, public shaming attempts to take on a humorous tone with sites specifically dedicated to shaming.

For instance, there are dog shaming sites where people put funny signs next to their dogs, such as, "I eat dirty Q-tips," or "I break into the pantry and hide potatoes all around the house." Meanwhile, there are other shaming sites that are meant to be funny but can be embarrassing for those being shamed. Some examples include the passenger shaming site that displays pictures of things people do while flying and the People of Walmart site that displays pictures of people wearing odd clothing or doing strange things in Walmart.

However, there are two types of public shaming that seem to occur more often than others, especially among teens. These include slut shaming and body shaming.

Slut Shaming

Slut shaming is a form of shaming where girls are targeted on social media and are humiliated for their sexuality. This means girls are

Slut shaming is a particularly vicious activity that involves the targeting and shaming of girls. Shamers make judgements about the girls' sexuality in written form that is distributed to the public.

often shamed for the way they look, the way they dress, and their presumed level of sexual activity.

Although the methods for shaming vary, public shamers often use social media sites to share explicit photos and videos. For instance, a shamer may post photos of a girl accompanied by rude or sexually explicit comments about her body. He or she also might engage in name-calling, such as labeling the girl a slut, whore, bimbo, tramp, or more.

For instance, in one slut shaming incident, the teens created several multipaned images and posted them to Instagram. One example included a picture of a girl with cleavage exposed and a caption that says, "Hey girls did you know that your boobs go inside your shirt?" Additionally, some high school students developed lists online called smut lists or slut lists.

Meanwhile, boys have been known to have sex with a girl and record it on their phone without her knowledge. Then, they share these videos with others as a way to shame and humiliate the girl. What they often don't realize is that if the girl is a minor, this is considered child pornography and they could be charged with a crime.

Sexting, which involves sharing nude or partially nude photographs through text messages, instant messaging, and e-mail, also contributes to slut shaming. There are many instances where a girl will share a nude or partially nude photo with a significant other while assuming the photo will be kept private. Then, after a breakup or just for fun, the boy will often share the photo with others. This photo then could be distributed many times and result in slut shaming for the girl.

Having or distributing nude or partially nude photos of a minor is against the law. Anyone with the photos in his or her possession, including the girl who took the photos, could be charged with a crime. Nude or partially nude photos of minors are considered child pornography.

No one can seem to escape body shaming. Even people in top shape can be ridiculed for being too physically fit and be accused of using performance-enhancing drugs or being too obsessed with themselves.

Body Shaming

Body shaming occurs when people make inappropriate or negative statements about another person's weight or size. This type of shaming impacts almost every body type. People are shamed for being thin. People are shamed for being overweight. People are even shamed for being too fit.

Basically, body shaming encompasses all words that people use to make someone feel bad about his or her body. When people engage in body shaming, they will either post pictures of someone online and shame the person for the way they look, or they will comment on selfies of a person with rude remarks about the person's body.

To a thin person, a shamer might say, "Gain some weight," and to an overweight person, he or she might say, "Lay off the hamburgers." Most of the time body shaming is directed at women and girls, but men can be victims, too. For instance, people might shame an overweight man for having "man boobs" or shame a physically fit man by insinuating that he is using steroids or growth hormones.

Recently, there has been a lot of backlash against body shaming. As a result, there is a movement online where people are trying to bring a more positive attitude toward diverse body sizes and types.

Is Public Shaming Free Speech?

Sometimes public shaming on the Internet can be more damaging than it is helpful. Years ago, public shaming worked in small communities. However, the vastness of the Internet has increased the amount of harm it can inflict. Would cracking down on shaming infringe on freedom of speech?

In the United States, freedom of speech is a big deal. It is one of our most prized freedoms. For example, the First Amendment prevents the government from punishing us for most speech. But free speech does come with responsibilities. While we all want to be heard, it is also important to do so appropriately.

For instance, there are certain types of speech that are prohibited, such as yelling "Fire!" in a crowded movie theater. Additionally, people cannot threaten to harm other people. Many times, depending on the state, this is against the law as well.

"Everyone thinks they can do anything they feel like doing online; [but] they can't," says Parry Aftab, an Internet privacy lawyer. "Free speech has its limits. If you defame somebody and you harass somebody, if you target them – that may be against the law."[14]

The important thing to remember when exercising your right to free speech is to do it in a way that allows you to communicate your message, your thoughts, and your ideas with respect for others.

While you can say almost anything without being arrested, this does not mean there won't be some social consequences for you. In other words, you may not have to go to jail for exercising your right to free speech, but this doesn't mean your friends will still want to hang out with you based on the rude things you post online.

3

Shame Comes at a Cost

Amanda Todd was only in seventh grade when she made a mistake that would haunt her for the next four years of her short life. Having just moved to a new area with her dad, Todd was hoping to meet new people, so she used video chat.

During the course of her conversations, she met people online that told her she was stunning and beautiful, which is something almost every awkward teenage girl wants to hear. But one of those people turned out to be an older man with the wrong intentions. He hounded her for a year to show him her breasts, and eventually in one impulsive move she gave in. This mistake would lead to years of stalking, slut shaming, cyberbullying, and name-calling as she moved from school to school trying to escape the shame.

Every time she moved, the man would find her. He would covertly become friends with kids at her school and people in her community by claiming he was a new student in the area and that he wanted to meet people. Then, he would contact Todd and threaten her. He told her if she did not put on a show for him, he would expose her photographs and ruin her life.[1]

"This man's intention, when he threatened Todd with exposure of the coercive images, was to slut shame Todd and make [her] feel like a whore," says Krissy Darch, a blogger for *Feminista*. "The weapon that this man was able to rely on was the judgment of our society . . . For a girl or woman, falling out of favor with her community can mean a sentence to a nightmarish cycle of distress."[2]

Todd's life definitely became a nightmare. As she moved from place to place, her stalker found her and shamed her each time. Just as he had predicted, people turned on her and joined in the public shaming for a mistake she made years earlier.

Every time she wouldn't give in to his demands, he would publicize her photos. At one point, he even created a Facebook page with her breasts as the profile picture. Instead of showing empathy or concern, her peers ostracized her and bullied her. People threatened her and posted cruel comments online. One boy even tricked her into believing he liked her, which led to his girlfriend and others beating her up and leaving her in a ditch. In a video describing her experience, Todd says: "I felt like a joke in this world . . . I thought nobody deserves this."[3]

Yet she could not escape the shame. In a stroke of desperation, she tried to kill herself by drinking bleach. However, she was rushed to the hospital and had her stomach pumped. People still did not stop tormenting her. They continued to shame her. They posted abusive messages about her failed suicide attempt. They blamed her and called her a slut and a whore despite the fact that an online predator more than twice her age was threatening and exploiting her.

Although Todd received counseling and took antidepressants, her life continued to spiral out of control. The shaming never ended. In October 2012, she could not take it any longer. Todd was found dead in her home—a tragic end of a young life brought on by a four-year shaming campaign.

Understanding Shame

Shame is that feeling people get when they feel like there is something terribly wrong with them. It is different from guilt. People feel guilty when they have done something wrong. People that feel shame believe there is something wrong with them at the core of who they are.

They also might feel inadequate, flawed, and humiliated. Shame is a deep gut-wrenching feeling that they are not worthy. When shame occurs on a public level, it can have devastating consequences. Suddenly, people's beliefs about themselves are no longer just feelings; they are reality. "The way in which [public shaming] impacts individuals fundamentally changes the arc of people's lives," says author and law professor Danielle Citron.[4]

With public shaming, there is permanence to the problem. Once humiliating information or photos are online, they never go away. Imagine what publicly shamed people, such as Amanda Todd, Monica Lewinsky, and countless others, would feel like thirty years later when a potential employer is evaluating them for a job and refuses to hire them based on an impulsive decision they made before the age of twenty-five. This level of public shame far exceeds what happened to shaming victims years ago.[5]

Today, people who are publicly shamed online find their lives in tatters afterward. They lose their jobs, friendships, and most importantly, their sense of dignity and self-worth. For some young people such as Amanda Todd or Tyler Clementi, a student at Rutgers who took his own life after his roommate shared video of him kissing another man, the rebuilding process is just too much, and they resort to suicide instead of trying to cope.

Suicide is not the only risk associated with public shaming. Other consequences include depression, anxiety, panic attacks, post-traumatic stress disorder, eating disorders, self-mutilation, and more.

Unfortunately for the people doing the shaming, they accomplish what they had hoped for. Shame makes the person on the receiving end feel like a "horrible person that is broken, worthless and disgusting," says Melissa Kirk, a researcher for a self-help psychology publisher.[6]

"Shaming, like sarcasm, is easy but damaging," Kirk says. "Brene Brown [a shame researcher] defines shame as 'the intense painful feeling or experience of believing we are flawed and therefore unworthy of acceptance and belonging.' We are probably wired to feel shame because it keeps us in line with the rules of our society." Kirk adds that when people break or flaunt rules, they may be ostracized, which can lead to feelings of disconnection. This disconnection can in turn feel worse than death "because people are wired to connect to and seek acceptance from others," she says.[7]

Shaming others makes people feel superior to another person, says Kirk. It also communicates to victims that others wish they would be different or act differently. When it is done online, people do not have to see the victim's face, the victim's reactions, or even take responsibility for their own feelings. "The same way teasing is . . . rooted in hostility, shame takes its energy from judgment and self-righteousness. Shame . . . is a way to control the other person by using their deeply ingrained need for connection to threaten them with disconnection."[8]

Highway to Hopelessness

People who have been publicly shamed frequently experience feelings of hopelessness and helplessness. Not only is their voice not heard over the roar of commenters and shamers online, but they also have no way to defend themselves.

This fact can leave targets of public shaming unable to concentrate or focus on anything in their life but the shaming. They are constantly distracted by their circumstances and the implications

The Rutgers University community memorialized Tyler Clementi after the first-year student killed himself from the shame of being spied on during a private sexual encounter with another man.

People who have been the targets of public shaming often find themselves unable to function because they can think of little else apart from the public's perception of them.

of the shaming. As a result, they are unable to function in other aspects of their lives, including keeping grades up, participating in activities, and communicating with family and friends.

"The [shamed] individual has sustained a massive loss of status in the world," says researchers Walter J. Torres, PhD, and Raymond M. Bergner, PhD. "[They] have been left without an effective voice to recover ... [and have] been branded and seen by others as unable even to read reality correctly . . . It is little wonder that the result would more often than not be profound feelings of worthlessness."[9]

There Are No Innocent Bystanders

There is nothing to be gained in watching another person being hurt. In fact, researchers have found that just observing social cruelty can have a psychological toll. According to Professor Ian Rivers at Brunel University in the UK, witnessing public shaming and bullying puts bystanders at an increased risk of self-harming behavior because of the significant impacts of watching another person be harmed. They feel powerless to help. What's more, he and his fellow researchers found higher rates of depression, substance abuse, and anxiety among students who had witnessed bullying. "The single most significant predictor of suicide risk among bystanders was found to be [feelings] of powerlessness," he says.[10]

Shamed to Death

Audrie Pott and Rehtaeh Parsons have something in common. They experienced slut shaming so severe that they felt they could no longer cope. Both girls committed suicide after nude or partially nude photos of them were made public and their peers tormented them with mean texts, tweets, and posts. While most experts indicate that suicide is a complicated issue with many facets to consider, suicide seems to be a frightening trend among teens that are attacked mercilessly online.

Take Audrie Pott as an example. She started her sophomore year at Saratoga High School two days after being sexually assaulted and photographed. As she walked the halls of her high school those first few days, photos of her both naked and explicitly decorated with Sharpie markers were being shared around school.

To make matters worse, she saw boys gathered together staring at their phones. She received hateful texts full of shaming words. Even a close friend confronted her in the hallway. Two days later, she hung herself.

It all started over Labor Day weekend. Pott told her mom she was sleeping over at a friend's house. But instead of just a quiet evening at home, the girls invited eleven other students to come over. After a night of heavy drinking, three boys and one girl helped Pott to a bedroom upstairs. Once in the room, the girl left, and the boys began pulling off her clothes and drawing on her with markers. With Pott still unresponsive, the boys also assaulted her and took pictures with their phones.

While it is hard to say if the photos of Audrie went viral or not, "she believed the images of her nearly naked body being fondled and abused without her consent were embedded in phones [everywhere]," writes Nina Burleigh in *Rolling Stone*. "[She believed] that it was only a matter of time before everyone she knew either saw [the photos] or knew what had happened to her body."[11]

"For raped and sexually assaulted young girls, it's one thing that people are gossiping about you in school," says Jeffrey Rosen, the Santa Clara County District Attorney, "but when you add images that they can keep forwarding, it really can seem like the whole world knows."[12]

As for fifteen-year-old Rehtaeh Parsons, she was gang-raped by four teenage boys at a house party near her home in Nova Scotia. She remembered only bits and pieces of what happened, including being led upstairs, vomiting, boys taking turns, and photos being taken. She was mortified when less than a week later, photos of the incident started to circulate at her school.

Even though she never returned to the school, she started receiving Facebook messages and texts with statements such as,

Unable to cope with the shame of being the subject of viral photos following her sexual assault, Audrie Pott took her life. Even though she was the victim, she was bullied and blamed for the incident.

"Sluts aren't welcome here," and "Everyone knows exactly what you have done." Meanwhile, men kept contacting her asking for sex. People she would pass on the street would murmur harassing words.

After seventeen months of shaming and bullying, Parsons hung herself. According to the journal *Child Abuse & Neglect,* half of youth who report dating violence and rape also report attempting suicide. Experts indicate that while rape is a heinous crime in itself, when the brutal moment is publicly shared with others, it compounds the psychological trauma.[13]

In fact, every two minutes a sexual assault happens in the United States, and nearly 50 percent of the victims are under the age of eighteen, according to Katherine Hull, a spokesperson for the Rape, Abuse, and Incest National Network (RAINN). High school- and college-aged women are at the highest risk for sexual assault.[14]

The Internet, smartphones, and social media have taken this crime to a whole new level. From Instagram and Snapchat to texting, today's young people with raging hormones and low impulse control are passing around pictures that shame young women.

Shame and Violence

James Gilligan, a psychiatrist and author who has worked with convicts, makes some interesting connections between shame and violence. In fact, based on his studies, he has observed a direct connection between violence and shame. He made these observations while serving as director for the Bridgewater State Hospital for the criminally insane and while director of mental health for the Massachusetts prison system.

Gilligan says he also discovered that all violent criminals were keeping a secret. "And that secret was that they felt ashamed—deeply ashamed, chronically ashamed, acutely ashamed," he explains. "I have yet to see a serious act of violence that was not provoked by the experience of feeling shamed or humiliated, disrespected and ridiculed."[15]

Spot the Signs of Suicide

Many times, teens attempt suicide because they are feeling hopeless, abandoned, alone, and rejected. They also may feel guilty or assume that they are a burden to others. They may also feel like they are out of options, and the thought of going through another day feels unbearable. These feelings are particularly relevant in teens who have been publicly shamed.

Although not everyone who attempts suicide displays warning signs in advance, many teens do. Make sure you are familiar with these red flags. Here is a list of things that could indicate a person is at risk for suicide.

- Appearing depressed or sad most of the time
- Talking about death or suicide
- Withdrawing from family and friends
- Losing interest in outside activities
- Displaying dramatic mood changes
- Acting erratic, reckless, or impulsive
- Changing eating or sleeping habits
- Expressing feelings of hopelessness and helplessness
- Indicating that his or her life is over or he or she is out of options
- Abusing drugs or alcohol
- Engaging in risky sexual behaviors
- Expressing feelings of guilt, remorse, or shame
- Getting in trouble at school or letting grades slip

If your friend displays any of these signs, you need to talk to a trusted adult right away. You also can call the National Suicide Prevention Hotline at 800-273-TALK (8255). Never ignore threats of suicide, signs of depression, or conversations about dying. Also never assume your friend is trying to get attention or acting like a baby. If he or she says or does something that just does not seem right, talk to someone about it right away. You are not gossiping about your friend. Telling someone could save his or her life.[16]

If you have a friend who abuses drugs or alcohol, reach out to help. He or she may be exhibiting warning signs for suicide. Talk to a trusted adult about how to get help for your friend.

Gilligan says that violent criminals often experienced many types of shame and violence growing up. For each of them, the shaming occurred at extreme and sometimes bizarre levels. Once grown up, "all the violence [was] the person's attempt to replace shame with self-esteem," he says.[17]

Gilligan adds that while "shame is initially painful, constant shaming leads to a deadening feeling." He compares it to feeling cold. "When [shame] reaches overwhelming intensity, [it] is experienced . . . as a feeling of numbness and deadness," he says. "[For example, in the book *Dante's Inferno*,] the lowest circle of hell was a region not of flames, but of ice—absolute coldness."[18]

4

Inside the Minds of Public Shamers

When Sam Biddle, a writer and editor for *Gawker*, posted Justine Sacco's tweet to his site, he wasn't hoping to ruin her career. He was taking advantage of a poorly worded tweet to drive traffic to the tech-industry blog he edited. His post read, "And Now, a Funny Holiday Joke from IAC's PR Boss" and listed her tweet that read, "Going to Africa. Hope I don't get AIDS. Just kidding. I'm white!"[1]

"It was a natural post," Biddle explains. "Twitter disasters are the quickest source of outrage, and outrage is traffic. I didn't think about whether or not I might be ruining Sacco's life . . . [But] the minimal post set off a 48-hour . . . eruption of Internet vindictiveness."[2]

Like he had hoped, his post went viral. Biddle received more than 230 comments to this single post. People were incensed with Sacco's careless remarks and called for her to be fired. Her employer had already communicated its displeasure, and major news outlets picked up the story.

Meanwhile, Sacco was on an eleven-hour flight and had no idea what was happening. Her phone was turned off, and no one could reach her. What's more, Twitter exploded with a new hashtag #HasJustineLandedYet. The angry mob of public shamers wanted to watch the drama unfold. "The furor over Sacco's tweet had become not just an ideological crusade against her perceived bigotry but also a form of idle entertainment," says Jon Ronson. "Her complete ignorance of her predicament for those eleven hours lent the episode both dramatic irony and a pleasing narrative arc."[3]

Sacco was in the air and unable to realize what she'd done or apologize for it. Several hours later, she got off the plane, into a social media nightmare, and was quickly fired from her job.

"Nearly as quickly, the righteous Twitter mob moved on," Biddle says. "Sacco-related hashtags went dark; blog posts were pushed down the page . . . and I didn't think much about Justine Sacco after that, either."[4] That is until he received an e-mail from her six months later. Suddenly, Biddle had to face what he had done—how his quest for more traffic on his site had ruined another person's life. "I realized suddenly that I felt very guilty about having . . . destroyed another person on what was basically a professional whim," Biddle explains.[5]

Although feeling anxious and uncertain, Biddle agreed to meet Sacco for dinner and drinks. What he discovered was that she wasn't anything like he had imagined. She was kind, friendly, and intelligent. She also explained the reason behind her tweet. Her trip made her think about how so many people consider HIV/AIDS an "African thing," when in reality the problem exists in the United States as well. She told Biddle that her tweet was meant to mimic what an actual racist, ignorant person would say.

But as with most jokes posted on the Internet, it fell flat. No one could see her face or hear her voice to know that she was being sarcastic and that she was joking. Complete strangers assumed simply by reading her tweet that they knew who she was and what she was like. And they jumped on it just like Biddle had done.

"Not knowing anything about her," Biddle explains, "I had taken [the tweet's] cluelessness at face value, and hundreds of thousands of people had done the same—instantly hating her because it's easy and thrilling to hate a stranger online."[6]

Months later, Biddle developed a newfound appreciation for what Justine Sacco must have felt. He, too, was being publicly shamed for a tweet he meant to be funny. "While sitting distracted and tired at my desk, riffing on the twisted online movement against 'social justice warriors' in video games, I wrote a tweet of my own," he says. The tweet read, "Ultimately #GamerGate is reaffirming what we've known to be true for decades: nerds should be constantly shamed and degraded into submission."[7] "Impulsively, and sort of laughing to myself, I added another [tweet], saying that we should 'Bring Back Bullying,'" he says. "It was insincere and over in an instant, to me at least."[8]

Hours later, hundreds of people had e-mailed Biddle and his editor. They challenged him and demanded he be fired. Meanwhile, he could not understand how they missed the joke. Quickly though, he realized there was nothing he could do now to change their opinions of him. "There wasn't any conversation to be had, no objective to reach or conclusion to draw," he explains. "Smashing a pinata isn't just for the candy—it *feels* great to swing your arms and feel a thud, and so they'd clobber me no matter what . . ."[9]

The Allure of Shaming

Jon Ronson, the author of *So You've Been Publicly Shamed,* has interviewed countless survivors of public shaming. He says that whenever possible, he tries to meet them in person to grasp the depth of their emotions and their experiences at the other end of the screen. What he found was a slew of broken people. "The people I met were mostly unemployed, fired for their transgressions and

It is all too easy to pile on the judging and shaming of others through the relative anonymity of social media. Doing so allows us to feel superior to those we perceive as being wrong.

they seemed broken somehow—deeply confused and traumatized," he says.[10]

Yet, the general public never sees this side of the person. They only see the mistake the person made through the glare of their screen. Meanwhile, the allure of anonymity and the adrenaline rush of shaming someone keeps them focused on a perceived need for justice. Even those like Ronson, who now advocate for more empathy online, have felt the power and rush that comes with shaming someone for wrongdoing.

"In the early days of Twitter, I was a keen shamer," admits Ronson. "When newspaper columnists made racist or homophobic statements, I joined the pile-on. Sometimes I led it . . . the collective fury felt righteous, powerful and effective."[11]

Ronson says that as time passed, though, he began to see a shift in shaming campaigns. No longer were they targeting just powerful institutions and public figures "but really anyone perceived to have done something offensive." For example, there have been several news stories about food service workers who wrote offensive comments on customer receipts, which the customers then posted online in an effort to shame the employee or restaurant. Ronson goes on to say, "I also began to marvel at the disconnect between the severity of the crime and the gleeful savagery of the punishment. It almost felt as if shamings were now happening for their own sake, as if they were following a script."[12]

Todd Wasserman, a writer on *Mashable,* a digital media website, agrees. "Constant access to social media has done some weird things to humanity," he says. "Our narcissism is off the charts, and with that comes a penchant for portraying ourselves as public crusaders." What's more, he suggests that public shaming is more about self-righteousness than exposing bad behavior. "The end result seems to be titillation rather than actual shaming," he says. "You read these tweets and you feel better about yourself because you're not one of those people."[13]

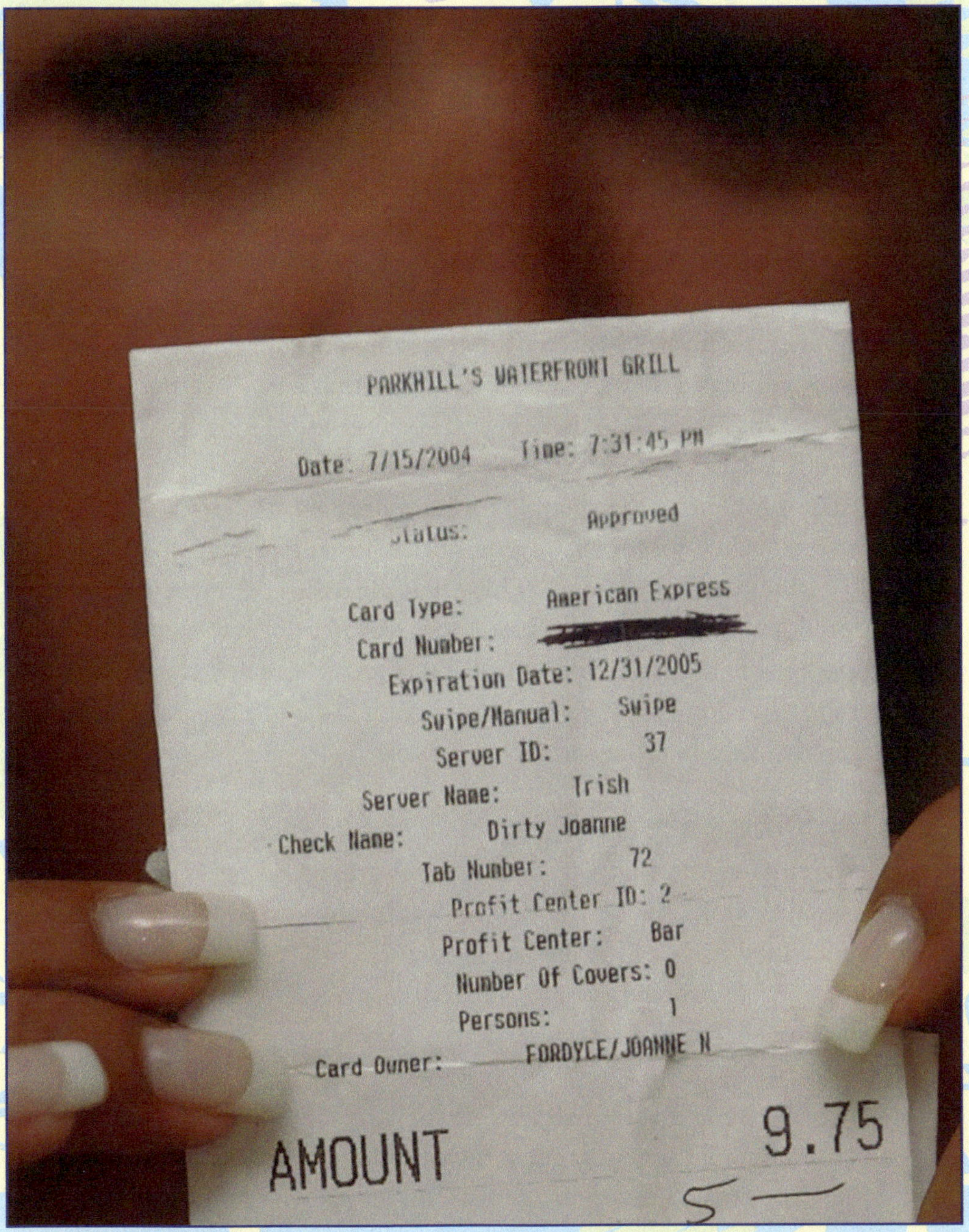

While we can agree this restaurant server was wrong to ridicule her customer, publicly shaming her is probably not as fair or as effective as complaining to her manager in person would have been.

People often believe they are doing the right thing by joining the mob. They feel like they are communicating to the others what is right and what is wrong. And somewhere in the back of their mind, they are hoping it will change the world—or at least the people being targeted. Shaming also gives people a sense of belonging when they join in with others.

"You show your proof of membership in a community by criticizing the most erratically," says Anil Dash, a tech entrepreneur and blogger who has been on the receiving end of racially charged Twitter mobs. "There's a social dynamic that says 'Let me show that I belong.' And there is a reward structure for being even more inflammatory."[14]

The problem is that people forget others are dimensional, says Ronson.[15] They forget that a one-dimensional tweet or post does not define another person. These people who are targeted and shamed are so much more than a few words on a screen. Lack of empathy is perhaps the biggest obstacle to recognizing this fact. It is impossible for people to see how their actions or posts have hurt someone else when they are behind a screen.

Throwing Stones: What Makes Them Do It?

Research suggests that the desire to see others suffer is a central personality trait. In fact, if you feel empathy for Amanda Todd, Monica Lewinsky, or Justine Sacco, chances are you were never the type to insult strangers online in the first place. If you find bullies, trolls, and shamers upsetting or offensive, you are probably not one of them.[16]

In fact, people who throw stones at others by publicly shaming and humiliating them may get some enjoyment out of what they are doing. They may be everyday sadists, or people who enjoy inflicting pain on others, according to Erin Buckels, a graduate student in psychology at the University of Manitoba. They are not criminals nor do they have a mental illness. They are just regular people who enjoy being cruel to other people.[17]

Buckels discovered this phenomenon in an experiment involving a bug-crunching machine. During the experiment, participants were given a choice between crunching live pill bugs named Muffin, Ike, and Tootsie or cleaning toilets and doing other unsavory chores. What she found is that people who scored high on measures of sadism by agreeing with statements such as, "I enjoy making jokes at the expense of others," were more likely to agree to killing the cleverly named bugs.[18]

To make the task as realistic as possible, she used a coffee grinder and rigged it to make grisly crunching sounds. Despite the gruesome sounds and cute bug names, she noted that sadistic participants

Sadly, some people derive enjoyment from making (and watching) others suffer. If you find yourself the target of these sadists, try not to show your pain; it only gives them more pleasure.

found the task pleasurable. The participants did not know that the bugs were not actually being crushed.

Buckels also found that the more sadistic people are, the more likely they are to go out of their way to make other people suffer. Moreover, public shamers, online trolls, and cyberbullies tend to have high sadism scores. Still, she's not completely sure why everyday sadists enjoy inflicting pain. "I don't know that they could answer that, to be honest," Buckels says. "They just find it pleasurable."[19]

Buckels also noticed that when targets speak out about their suffering, it likely only adds to their tormentors' glee. "It increases the enjoyment when they see they've affected some kind of horrible outcome on someone," she says. "If they don't get to see it, it's less pleasurable."[20]

Before You Cast the First Stone

The next time you notice someone behaving poorly online—whether they are making poor jokes at another's expense, expressing hate toward people, or are behaving in a way that you disagree with—think twice. Before you cast that first stone and let them know what you really think, stop and remember that there is a human being on the other side of the screen.

This does not mean bad behavior should never be addressed. It absolutely should be. But there is much debate about whether or not public shaming is the best way to address inappropriate actions. Additionally, some experts argue it does not even accomplish what the shamers hope it will—a change in behavior.

While you may feel empowered and anonymous and truly believe what they did is wrong, it is still not a good idea to hurt another person on such a grand scale. Remember, public shaming often results in severe consequences that far exceed the initial infraction. There is also a chance in your quest for justice that you are, in fact, creating an injustice.

Surround yourself with positive people who will support you and be happy for your successes. These are the people who will feel sympathy and offer help when you are feeling down.

Five Reasons Why Teens Publicly Shame

Public shaming is a growing problem that impacts people every day. The reasons behind public shaming can run the gamut from anger and revenge to longing to fit in. Here is an overview of the top five reasons why teens publicly shame others.

They believe the target deserves it. When someone makes a mistake online or in public, people often feel justified in publicizing it to the world along with a few rude comments. After all, they want the person to realize that what he or she did is unacceptable, and now the whole world knows about it. Whether it is a minor infraction, such as refusing to leave a tip or taking someone's parking spot, or a larger offense, such as making derogatory comments about women at a computer conference, people feel justified in humiliating other people. Consequently, they usually do not feel remorse or guilt for publicly shaming someone if they feel the target deserves it.

They want to alleviate boredom. Teens who are bored or looking for entertainment will sometimes join in on public shaming to spice things up or add some excitement and drama to their lives. For many teens, the Internet is their only source of entertainment. It also becomes an outlet for getting attention and gaining followers or likes to a page or post.

They are hungry for power. Public shaming is a way for kids to feel powerful. They look at those who are being shamed and are thankful they are not that person. They feel good about themselves because they are in a position that can bring another person to his or her knees. For some teens, it is a rush to be able to make another person feel ashamed, alone, and humiliated. What's more, engaging in public shaming is a way for them to gain some social power.

They believe they won't get caught. The anonymity of the Internet gives teens a false sense of security. They believe if they post things anonymously that they won't get caught or that no one will realize who it is. What's more, teens who publicly shame others do not necessarily see the reaction of the victim, which makes it easy to say and do things they wouldn't do in person. In fact, a significant number of kids who are not otherwise confrontational will engage in public shaming because the Internet makes them feel empowered.

They lack empathy. Most kids who publicly shame others believe it is not a big deal. In fact, many times students who engage in public shaming do not feel bad about what they are doing. They do not realize that the person on the receiving end is suffering. Instead, publicly shaming other people makes them feel funny, popular, and powerful.

5

Keeping Shaming at Bay

Lindsey Stone and her friend Jamie Schuh enjoyed taking ridiculous pictures. It was kind of their thing. For instance, they might take a picture of the two of them smoking in front of a No Smoking sign. Or maybe they would take a picture in front of statue mimicking its pose.

But when Stone posed for a picture in front of the Silence and Respect sign at Arlington National Cemetery, she never imagined the reaction she would get. Instead of causing a laugh and a few disgruntled remarks from friends, the photo of her staged to look like she was yelling while making an inappropriate gesture found its way around the Internet.

Schuh had posted the picture to Facebook and tagged Stone with her permission. Yet even when their friends expressed their dislike, Stone left the photo up and posted a comment instead. "Whoa whoa whoa . . . wait," Stone wrote on her Facebook page. "This is just us

Lindsey Stone's life was turned upside down after she posted a harmless photo on social media. Her public shaming spread like wildfire, leading to the loss of her job and a bout of depression.

being the douchebags that we are, challenging authority in general. Much like the pic posted the night before, of me smoking right next to a no smoking sign. OBVIOUSLY we meant NO disrespect to people that serve or have served our country."[1]

But the rest of the country did not see it that way. Despite being posted on her private Facebook page, Stone's photo reached the general public, and the public was outraged. A former service member created a Facebook page called "Fire Lindsey Stone," and a Change.org petition to get her fired was developed. Meanwhile, major news outlets began covering the story while Stone's photo started circulating the Internet on a broader scale. Her life as she knew it was about to come to an end.[2]

Even after she was fired, people did not relent. A "Set Fire to Lindsey Stone" group was created on Facebook. Some commenters suggested that she should be shot, while others wanted her exiled from the United States. Despite having issued an apology and explaining that while inappropriate, the photo was simply a poor joke among friends, people did not give in. They were having too much fun. Stone did not show her face much after that.[3]

"Literally overnight, everything I knew and loved was gone," Stone says.[4] After the shaming, she became depressed. She couldn't sleep, and she barely left her home for a year. She felt like she could never just be happy and relaxed. "[Public shaming] really impacts the way you view the world," she says.[5]

How to Avoid Being Publicly Shamed

No one wants to find him or herself in a situation like Lindsey Stone, where he or she has made a tasteless joke online that suddenly the whole world knows about, but it can happen quickly and easily if the wrong person sees it and decides to run with it. There are also other activities that can lead to shaming, such as sexting, oversharing, and selfies.

While shaming can happen anywhere online, it is especially prevalent on Facebook and Twitter. In fact, Twitter is a fast machine

Post Selfies With Care

Taking and posting selfies is something almost every teen likes to do. It is a fun way to document how you spend your time and to tell others about your day. But to reduce the risks of public shaming, it is important to pay close attention to your selfies.

For instance, keep in mind what you are wearing, what you are doing, and what is in the background. Remember, every aspect of a picture communicates a message about who you are. Here are some other things to remember about selfies.

Selfies can be altered. Keep in mind that public shamers and trolls can use different types of software programs and apps to alter photos. One common thing that is done is to take a headshot and put it on another body. Or a shamer might superimpose an object into the picture. In general, once a selfie is on the Internet, you lose control over how the photo can be used.

Selfies can be shared. Remember that once a photo is on the Internet, even if only for a minute, it can be downloaded and shared multiple times over. Another way in which selfies are shared is by taking screenshots of the photo and sharing. Even photos in popular apps, such as Snapchat, in which photos are supposed disappear in a matter of seconds, are able to be copied and shared. As a result, it is important to remember that once you post a selfie, there is no way to really remove it from the Internet.

Selfies should be kept private. Be sure you have made all your social media accounts as private as possible. Block any known bullies, trolls, or public shamers from your accounts. You also should be sure that the geotagging services on your smartphone are turned off. People can use that data to find out where you are.[6]

that almost begs for misunderstanding, says Sam Biddle, the writer for *Gawker* who posted Justine Sacco's tweet about Africa and AIDS. His repost of her tweet led to her being fired. Later, he was ridiculed for a tweet he posted about bullying. "The same flatness of affect that can make [Twitter] such a weird and funny place also makes it a tricky and dangerous one," says Biddle. "Jokes are complicated, context is hard. Rage is easy."[7]

The best thing you can do to avoid becoming a victim of public shaming is to be careful about what you post. Try to avoid posting anything inflammatory or that could be taken out of context. You

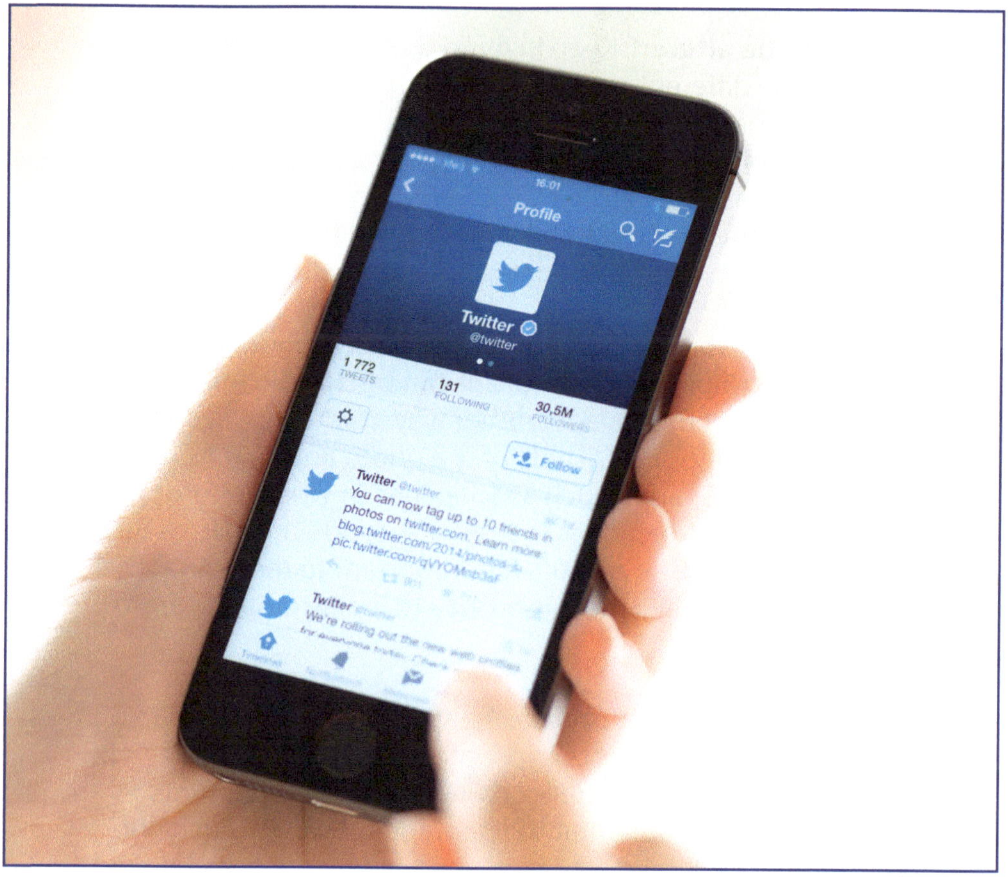

Twitter can be a tricky medium to navigate. Due to its character limitations, Twitter encourages quick, shallow quips. These can easily be read as inflammatory, even when they're not intended to be.

also should proof your texts and tweets before clicking. Make sure they cannot be misinterpreted. Here is a list of other precautions you can take to avoid being publicly shamed.

Save the jokes for face-to-face conversations. Much like Justine Sacco, Sam Biddle, and even Lindsey Stone realized, one poorly worded joke can turn your life upside down and haunt you for years to come. Be sure to avoid posting jokes online. When people cannot see your face or hear your voice, it is easy for a joke to be misinterpreted, especially by people who do not know you. Stick to positive posts rather than trying to be funny. Rarely do people get jokes made online.

Avoid sexting. Sexting is something no teen should be participating in. Aside from the fact that sending and receiving nude (or even half-nude) pictures is considered child pornography, it also can lead to serious public shaming that is hard to undo. Think about Amanda Todd's story. One topless picture ruined her life. Even if you think the person you are sending the photos to is going to keep them confidential, you have no way of knowing. In one click of a button, your intimate photo can be shared with the entire world.

Limit the number of selfies you take. While there is nothing wrong with taking the occasional selfie, posting a lot of them online can put you at a greater risk for public shaming. This is especially true if your selfies are meant to be funny like Lindsey Stone had hoped her selfie would be. One selfie in the wrong place at the wrong time can cause a lot of damage. Be sure when you are taking selfies that you consider what you are doing, as well as what is in the photo. For instance, if you are the president of Students Against Drunk Driving and you are having dinner with your parents at a restaurant bar and snap a photo, people could take that photo out of context and try to publicly shame you. Remember, take selfies with care, and limit the number you post.

Think before you post. Before you click the button to post, tweet, or share something, stop and think about it. Ask yourself if this comment could be taken out of context or misinterpreted by

To avoid public shame, be a responsible social media participant. Take a second to consider how your post could be interpreted by others. What's funny to you might offend someone else.

someone else. Try to look at what you are posting, tweeting, and sharing from all points of view. Be sure that what you are posting would not hurt another person in some way. The problem with Lindsey Stone's photo is that it offended and hurt a number of servicemen and servicewomen. It also offended people who had lost friends and family members to war because her photo was taken in front of the Tomb of the Unknown Soldier.

Avoid oversharing. It is easy to provide too much information on the Internet either in posts or profiles. As a teen, it is critically important that you do not give away too much personal information, such as which school you attend, your home address, your place of employment, and so on. Doing so puts you at risk for predators to easily find you. Additionally, you want to avoid oversharing your thoughts, opinions, and emotions. These are the types of things that public shamers use against people. It is best to keep these things off the Internet. You want to do what you can to protect your online reputation because colleges and future employers often research those they are considering. Be sure everything they read about you online is positive and puts you in a good light.

Be extra careful if you are a female. There appears to be a trend among public shamers to make rape and death threats to females specifically. According to Jon Ronson, author of *So You Have Been Publicly Shamed,* shamers are "breathtakingly misogynistic." What this means is that a number of shamers show a dislike or hatred toward women and girls. According to Ronson, when Justine Sacco "stepped out of line, the rape threats were instant."[8]

Steer clear of trolls. If you encounter a person online who makes inflammatory comments about one of your posts or tweets, it is best to block that person right away. You also should consider reporting him or her to the social media platform you are using. Most importantly, do not engage with a troll. Trolls are looking to start conflict online, and communicating with them only makes the situation worse. Creating negative feelings and getting a reaction from you is exactly what they want. Do not give it to them.

One of the great pleasures of having a smartphone is the ability to take selfies. Be aware of the image you're projecting, however. Even the most innocent photo is fair game for some Internet trolls.

Google your name. It is always a good idea to put your name into Google and see what pops up. You want to be sure the things that pop up when someone searches for your name show you in a positive light. Additionally, every month or so, you should look through your pictures and your posts to be sure everything out there is positive. Delete anything that could be misinterpreted. You should also check your privacy settings to be sure your photos and posts are as protected as they can be online. Remember, colleges and future employers will likely Google your name. Be sure you know what they will find.

Avoid posting to social media or texting when you are upset. Nothing is more dangerous than posting a comment or tweeting when you are angry, hurt, or upset. Sometimes your emotions can get the best of you, and you could say something that you might regret later. The problem with social media, though, is that once it is out there, there is no way to get it back. Make it a rule of thumb to put your phone down and close your computer when you are feeling angry, frustrated, or sad. It is never a good idea to use social media when you are experiencing strong emotions. Wait until your head has cleared before you use social media. It is also a good rule of thumb to avoid posting about emotional topics any way.

Sticks and Stones: Managing Your Online Reputation

Most parents tell their kids not to worry about what people say about them. For the most part, this is pretty good advice, but when it comes to the Internet, it is important to remember that it has a much longer reach than mean words and gossip in the school community.

One of the best ways to combat rumors, gossip, and even public shaming is to build a positive online reputation that crowds out negative search results. The goal is to create positive content that will rank higher in a Google search than any of the negative stuff. Begin by creating a positive social media presence. For instance, consider purchasing a domain name with your name. You do not have to build a website yet, but owning it keeps others from snatching it up.

Blogs are another way to build a positive online presence if managed appropriately. Pick a topic that you are passionate about and blog about it. Just be sure to consider how teachers, college administrators, and future employers might view it. Some blog ideas include highlighting service projects teens can participate in, reviewing books or movies, offering healthy eating options on a teen budget, or demonstrating how to excel in school. Here are a few more ideas on to manage your online reputation.

Learn how to use social media to your advantage. Be sure to promote the goals you achieve, milestones you attain, and anything else that puts you in a positive light. If you feel like it is bragging, have your parents post it and tag you in it. The goal is that the positive things you have achieved will show up when colleges and recruiters Google your name. It is also important to keep a record of anytime you make the news or are mentioned in a newspaper. For example, if your name is mentioned in the local paper because of an athletic achievement, a charity you support, or an academic honor, keep a list of these things. This recognition can be used on applications and promoted in social media.

Publish quality online content. Develop a blog or make videos for YouTube that are of interest to others and related to your potential career path. Another option is to find a charity, cause, or service project that you are passionate about. Then, develop content around that. Not only does this help prevent public shaming, but it also looks great on a college application, especially if you do a good job and get positive reviews. Also, be sure you have firm control over the comment sections of your pieces. You may want to review comments before they are posted to your pieces or not allow comments at all.

Manage your online reputation. There may be a great deal of references about you online in which you are not the original poster. These posts might include photos your friends tagged you

Being connected to the virtual world can be lots of fun, but it also comes with some potential dangers. It is essential that you be vigilant in managing your online reputation.

Be Smart About Smartphones

A number of tweens and teens today have smartphones. In fact, according to the Pew Internet & American Life Project, 25 percent of teens between the ages of fourteen and seventeen have a smartphone.[9] While you may know how to use your phone responsibly, staying within the guidelines of your data plan and not accessing inappropriate material online, there are some activities that can put you at risk for public shaming. Here are a few things to keep in mind.

FaceTime and other video chat options should be used with caution. Keep in mind that anytime you use FaceTime or other visual chatting options, the person on the other side of the screen can snap a photo of you anytime he or she wants and upload it to a social media account. As a result, teens have been caught making embarrassing gestures, wearing revealing clothing, or doing something inappropriate. Sometimes taking and posting these photos is meant to be funny and harmless, but if the wrong person gets a copy of the photo, it can lead to public shaming.

Your smartphone is not community property. Many teens pass their smartphone off to a friend to use without a second thought. While letting someone use your phone to call a parent is a kind and generous thing to do, you do not have to let your friends use your phone every time they ask. Keep in mind that they are using your data if they are using the Internet capabilities. If they are sending texts from your phone, it looks like you sent the text.

A well-meaning friend might text something inappropriate from your phone, and if someone questions it later, there is no way to prove that you did not send the text. After all, it came from your phone. Additionally, when you hand your phone over to a friend, he or she can access your social media accounts. While most of the time being hacked on social media is harmless, if your friend posts something inappropriate, it could end up creating problems for you. You need to take steps to protect your accounts, your phone, and your private information.

People can take pictures even if your phone is password protected. On the iPhone, a user can simply swipe the camera icon and snap a picture. He or she does not have to know the password or even unlock the phone. It is common in a group of friends to grab another person's phone and start snapping pictures. However, there are times when kids will use another person's phone to snap embarrassing or inappropriate photos. Later, when scrolling through the photos, you might be shocked at what you find. As a result, never put your phone down and walk away. If photos of body parts, people using the restroom, or locker-room shots show up on your phone, you will be the one held responsible.

in or references to you made by others. To keep track of what others are posting, do a search once a month and check for questionable posts and photos. Remove tags from photos of you that do not represent the image you want online, or ask your friends to remove the photos. Send requests to website moderators and social media networks requesting that anything questionable be removed if you are not able to get the person to remove it. Sites such as Instagram and Facebook will investigate posts, especially when they pertain to minors.

Join networking sites. When you are older, look into joining LinkedIn and other professional networking sites to develop relationships with adults in your field. You also may hear about scholarships, internships, and other opportunities through these networking tools. It also demonstrates to college recruiters and future employers a level of maturity and interest in the professional world.

Remember, your online reputation is a valuable asset, and if handled properly, it can open doors and impact your future. Focus on building a solid reputation now, and you will have a head start on success.

6 What You Can Do If You Have Been Publicly Shamed

Every day we hear more stories about public shaming. For instance, not too long ago Iggy Azalea (pictured above) was shamed about her body. *Fashion Police* cohost Giuliana Rancic shamed actress Zendaya for her hairstyle at the Oscars before being s hamed for her shaming. Meanwhile, Justin Bieber always seems to be shamed about something.

Luckily for them, these are celebrities. They have public relations teams to help them navigate through shaming campaigns. They also push the good stuff they do to the top of Internet search engines. The average American is not so fortunate.

"We may think it's tough to be a celebrity, having everything one does—good, bad or anything in between—go viral. But it's even tougher *not* to be, if you post something negative online. Because when you're not a celebrity, it seems only bad stuff goes viral, not just every little thing you do," says Anne Collier, founder of Net Family

News, a nonprofit organization that focuses on Internet safety and youth-related technology.[1]

"A stupid joke, a callous remark, a cranky critical comment gets posted, and the non-celebrity can suddenly find him or herself judged by thousands or by millions," she says. "The public has no context, and so somehow you're *defined*—either intentionally by someone who has it in for you or by a public seeking entertainment on a slow news day—by something bad you mindlessly or angrily said."[2]

Getting Your Life Back

If you have been publicly shamed, you are likely feeling a wide range of emotions, including everything from sadness and anger to regret and disbelief. Some days it may feel like you will never get back to normal. You long for the days before the shaming began when life was much simpler and the world didn't make threats and disparaging jokes at your expense. Here are seven things you can do that will help you get on the road to recovery.

Keep Shaming in Perspective

It's normal to experience a wide variety of emotions ranging from intense humiliation and sadness to anger and regret after being publicly shamed, says Amy Morin. Morin is a psychotherapist, About.com's Parenting Teens and Child Discipline Expert, and author of the best seller *13 Things Mentally Strong People Don't Do*. It's also important not to suppress or ignore those feelings, she says.[3]

"Allow yourself to feel those things—just make sure you don't get stuck there," Morin says. "If your emotions start to interfere with your ability to function—your grades suffer, you isolate yourself, or you aren't able to fulfill your daily responsibilities—it's important to take steps to regulate your emotions in a healthy way."[4]

Morin says the best way to change how you feel is to change how you think and behave. Be on the lookout for thoughts that may

If you have experienced public shaming, do your best to prevent it from damaging your life. Although you can't change what has happened, you can change your perspective.

exaggerate your current situation and work to change your thought patterns. "Although you may be experiencing tough circumstances, don't convince yourself that your entire life is ruined. Reframe those overly negative thoughts into something more realistic."[5] For instance, instead of focusing on what happened to you and dwelling on what others are saying, start thinking about where you want to go from here. Ask yourself if there is a way to turn this negative situation into something positive.

Meanwhile, to keep things in perspective, you also need to work on changing your behavior. As tempting as it is to hole up inside your home, this is not always a healthy option. Instead, try something new, get together with safe friends, or start an exercise regime. The point is to get up and get moving, says Morin. "Instead of sitting on the couch . . . or isolating yourself [try] socializing with your closest friends," she says. "Sometimes, it's important to go out and do something even when you don't feel like it."[6] Get involved in activities that will distract you from rehashing and replaying hurtful words or events in your mind over and over again.

Change Your Thought Processes

Many times, people who have been publicly shamed will dwell on what they have experienced and allow it to consume their every thought. The goal is that your thoughts revolve around things that have meaning or purpose in your life and not the shaming you experienced.

"Changing your thoughts can help motivate you to keep moving forward even on the days where you don't feel like it," says Morin. "That may mean going to school, even when you really don't want to, or going to basketball practice on a day where you just don't think you can do it. Treat yourself like a trusted friend by practicing some self-compassion . . . your kind words to yourself can help you recover from the pain."[7]

Morin also suggests challenging your thoughts. For instance, she says if you think thoughts such as, "The whole world knows

When you find yourself moping around the house, going over and over what has happened to you, turn to activities that will stop your brain from obsessing. A tough workout can help quiet your mind.

what people are saying," getting out of the house can help you see that your thought is exaggerated. Once out of the house, you will see that there are plenty of people who have no idea what is going on.[8]

If you have trouble changing your thought processes on your own, a counselor may be able to help you redirect your thoughts. Remember, you need to look for the lessons in public shaming and leave the negative stuff behind.

Do Not Embrace Victim Thinking

The key to recovering from public shame is that you do not allow what happened to you to define who you are as person. Instead, practice gratitude, suggests Morin. "It's impossible to feel sorry for yourself and experience gratitude at the same time," she says. "Identify at least three things every day you have to be grateful for. Even simple things, like the warm sunshine or a cool breeze, are reason enough to feel grateful."[9]

Morin also suggests that victims of public shaming should refuse to feel sorry for themselves. "While it is OK to feel sad, hosting your own pity party will only make things worse. Acknowledge the hardship that you are facing, but make a conscious decision not to get dragged down by self-pity."[10] Finally, Morin urges people who have been publicly shamed not to give away their power. "Don't let people who have shamed you define who you are. Refuse to let them control how you think, feel, and behave," she says. "Make decisions based on who you are and who you want to be, not who others say you are."[11] Leave the hurtful words and actions in the past. Instead, recognize your strengths and develop those. Remember, there is so much more that you have to offer. The public shaming you experienced does not define you.

Get Mentally Tough

"It's much easier to be mentally strong when everything is going well in life," says Morin. "But the true test of mental strength comes when you encounter hardship."[12] Public shaming can easily take an emotional toll. Taking steps to regulate your thoughts, manage your

The best antidote to being judged and criticized by a mob of strangers online is to spend time with your friends. Having fun with a group of people who love you will remind you of who you really are.

emotions, and behave productively despite your circumstances will boost your mental strength, says Morin.

Remember, asking for help is not a sign of weakness. "In fact, it's a sign of strength and shows you want to take action to improve your situation," says Morin. "Don't hesitate to ask a trusted adult for help when you are struggling."[13]

Reclaim Control

Feelings of powerlessness and helplessness are common among victims of public shaming and can carry over into other areas of life. As a result, you run the risk of living your life as a perpetual victim. "You can't control what other people say about you, and you can't control who believes the information," says Morin. "But you can control how you react. Put your energy into being a person of character, and worry less about what other people think of you."[14]

This also helps to identify things in your life that you do have control over. For instance, you can choose to think about something other than the shaming. Or you can choose to do something to help others in similar situations. The point is that you learn how to identify healthy choices and follow through with them. Doing so will help you feel more in control of your life.

You also should forgive yourself for mistakes that you may have made, says Morin. "Don't beat yourself up over something that happened in the past. Instead, decide that you're going to learn from it, and move on. Trying to punish yourself will only make things worse."[15]

Focus on Personal Growth

When it comes to growing and learning from this experience, it is important to identify areas where you may need to grow and heal. For instance, public shaming can shatter a person's self-esteem. If you find yourself feeling insecure or uncertain about who you are, look for ways to build your self-esteem by focusing on something you are good at.

Dos and Don'ts of Public Shaming

When it comes to public shaming, everyone is fair game. Even if you stay out of drama at school and try not to post anything inflammatory online, it doesn't guarantee that public shamers will not target you. After all, it only takes one poorly worded joke on Twitter to wreak havoc on a person's life. If you ever find yourself in a public shaming situation, here are seven things to remember.

Don't respond. The best way to respond to public shaming is to ignore the posts and comments. Although it is difficult to refrain from responding to something so painful or at least trying to explain what you were thinking, do not respond. Even an apology can keep the shaming cycle running. The idea is to let the story die out.

Don't obsess about what you read. Continuing to think about what others are saying is not healthy. It steals your time and your energy. Plus, it only makes you feel worse. Try to focus on other things. Plan outside activities, get together with friends, or take a trip to take your mind off what is being said online.

Don't read the comments. Once you know that people are publicly shaming you, you need stop reading the posts and the comments. Although it is natural to wonder what others are saying about you, it is not always a good idea. Instead, focus on things you can control, and try to stay off the Internet and social media for a while.

Don't pursue revenge. Remember, seeking revenge is not a healthy response to online shaming. In fact, any communication with the shamers, including attempting to shame them in return, is rewarding their efforts and keeping the cycle moving. As long as public shamers get a response, they will continue.

People will lose interest in the public shaming much more quickly if you do nothing in response.

Don't lose hope. Public shaming can feel overwhelming and devastating, but remember this experience will not last forever. While it is tough to deal with the consequences, you can get through it. Stay focused on the future, your goals, and your dreams, and do not let this situation define you.

Do take down your social media accounts. Sometimes the best response to public shaming is to close all your social media accounts. Once the shaming has died down, you can open new accounts with slightly different account names. For instance, you do not want to use the same Twitter handle that you had when you were shamed. Change it somewhat so people do not start the shaming again.

Do post positive things online. Once you have experienced public shaming, it is important to change your online reputation. Sometimes the best way to do that is to develop positive blog posts, websites, and other tools that push the negative search results down. Also, it is crucial to be careful about anything and everything you post to avoid giving the shamers ammunition to start the shaming campaign all over again.

Meanwhile, if assertiveness is an issue for you, take a class or read a book that helps you gain tools for becoming more assertive. Or if you struggle with anxiety or have panic attacks every time you go online, find a counselor or a doctor that can help you work through those issues. The goal is to identify areas in your life that you need to work on.

Find Closure for the Shaming

Part of the healing process is being able to put the past behind you and detach from the trauma you experienced. Sometimes this happens naturally as the shaming dies down and the online community moves on to something else. Other times, it will take a little more creativity. The goal is that you no longer allow your thoughts to be preoccupied with what happened to you.

Don't underestimate the severity of how public shaming can affect you. If you find yourself unable to cope, seek help from a friend, family member, teacher, or counselor. One incident should not define the rest of your life.

Reverse the Shaming

There are reputation management companies, such as Reputation .com, that specialize in online reputation management. While it is a high-priced alternative for dealing with public shaming, these companies have some success. They flood the Internet with positive posts and pictures in an attempt to push the negative search results down the page.

Jon Ronson, author of *So You've Been Publicly Shamed,* convinced Reputation.com to work with Lindsey Stone. The goal was to reduce how often the picture of Stone in front of the Silence and Respect sign appeared in search results for her name.

As a result, the company created blog posts and other online information that were innocent and boring. The approach worked to some degree—her Google results show more of her positive attributes and less of the infamous photo. "We were creating a world where the smartest way to survive is to be bland," Ronson says.[16]

7

How to End Shaming for Good

Shame is a powerful thing. Just look at how public shaming impacted Monica Lewinsky, Justine Sacco, Lindsey Stone, Amanda Todd, and countless others. Most of us would do anything to avoid shame like what they experienced, including sometimes siding with shamers, trolls, and bullies rather than standing up for the victims.

"Shame is contagious, and we fear that if we are associated with the victim, we will be tarred with the same brush and subjected to the same humiliation," says Brock Hansen LCSW, a psychotherapist and author of *Shame and Anger: The Criticism Connection*. "The problem with shaming through the Internet is that the victim has no way of effectively confronting the abusive shamers. It's not a fair fight."[1]

However, the end result is painful humiliation and real damage to the victim's reputation and image, Hansen says. "Some victims have committed suicide [like Amanda Todd], seeing no future for themselves in a world where devastating images can be published on the Internet forever by people they don't even know."[2]

But are you truly powerless to help? Hansen says that standing up for the victim instead of piling on with the others is a good first step. It takes a great deal of courage, but it can go a long way in combating the feelings of helplessness you may feel when you witness public shaming. Having the courage to question public shaming is something you should feel good about, he says, "even if it does not stop the phenomenon." What's more, the more defenders that participate in the conversation, the less lopsided the public shaming will be. Standing up for another person comes with some risks though.[3]

"In fact, [public shamers] can be shamed, too, and often retaliate with greater rage when they are," Hansen says. "When one person takes a highly critical position and another pushes back, the first person frequently becomes defensive and more aggressive." So be prepared and be careful when confronting public shaming.[4]

Jump off the Bandwagon

Empathy may, in fact, be the key to putting an end to public shaming. If you can stop and tune into your feelings of empathy or your ability to understand how it might feel to be in someone else's shoes, you might be able to understand how painful it is to hear shaming words from people you do not even know.

According to Mike Robbins, a motivational speaker and author of *Focus on the Good Stuff* and *Be Yourself, Everyone Else Is Already Taken*, empathy is different from sympathy and pity. It also does not involve agreement, commiseration, or endorsement. "Simply put, empathy is getting into another person's world and connecting with them both emotionally and compassionately," Robbins says. "We don't have to agree with them or fully understand them to be able to empathize. We don't even need to be able to relate to what they are experiencing specifically. We just need to . . . connect with them where they are, and acknowledge what they're experiencing."[5]

Robbins says most people have trouble being empathetic because they allow their egos, opinions, and judgments to get in way of their ability to express empathy. "If I agree with someone completely, can totally relate to them, and see things exactly as they do; it's quite easy for me to empathize with them," he explains. "However, if I don't agree, can't relate, have a very different take on the situation or actually think how they're reacting to things is potentially harmful for them and others, it's often very hard for me to be empathetic toward them and I also worry that my expression of empathy could come across as agreement or endorsement."[6]

This is especially true with public shaming. It is hard to feel empathetic toward someone who is behaving in way that we find appalling. This is why it is easy for people to jump on the bandwagon and join in on the public shaming. But if we want to stop seeing people's lives ruined for making public mistakes, we are going to have to jump off the bandwagon and resolve to behave more compassionately online.

"Shaming is self-righteousness masquerading as social justice," adds Cole Stryker, author of *Hacking the Future* and *Epic Win for Anonymous*. "In many cases, the targets [may] deserve to be exposed . . . but public shaming does not drive social progress. It might make us feel better, but let's not delude ourselves into thinking we've made a positive difference."[7]

As a result, if you want to see public shaming become less of an issue, start by resolving not to harm other people, and turn off the instinct to shame others. Practice the art of thinking about what you want to say online before you say it. If you feel disgust, anger, or hurt, step away from the computer. More often than not, the words you are about to type are neither helpful nor kind. Remember, there are fellow human beings with feelings and lives behind those tweets, posts, texts, comments, and images that make you angry. Here are additional things you can do to put an end to public shaming.

Do not pile on. When you see a group of people online shaming another person, avoid the urge to add your two cents to the conversation. Even if you feel the person is wrong and deserves to be told, do not add to the shaming. More often than not, the consequences of shaming outweigh the online offense. As a result, it is always best to practice restraint.

Stick up for the victim. If you see someone being shamed online, consider sticking up for him or her. Like Hansen said, you do not have to agree with the person being shamed to show empathy and treat the victim like a human being. Even just one positive comment can go a long way in providing hope that there is still good in this world.

Refuse to read gossip or shaming posts, blogs, and tweets. Every time you retweet, comment on, or even read the public shaming one person is doing to another, you are giving that person power to hurt another human being. The best thing you can do is to ignore people that shame others. If they are not able to increase traffic, gain more likes, or create a following from shaming others, they will be less likely to do it.

Flood social media with positivity. There is too much negative stuff in cyberspace. Instead of chiming in about who did this or who is doing that, make sure your posts are positive and encouraging. You could even develop your own hasthtag, such as #EndShaming or #ShamingIsNotCool. Be creative, and come up with a way to change the conversation.

Avoid liking posts that shame others. If one of your friends shames another classmate on Instagram, do not like that post. Even if you do not make a comment to the post, simply liking it gives it power. Instead consider sticking up for the victim, blocking the sender, or unfriending the sender. All of these actions communicate that you think shaming is uncool.

Even if you have not personally been the target of public shaming, there are things you can do to avoid it. One is to step away from your computer or device and have face-to-face interactions.

Stop Fighting Monsters

The more we click on gossip, rumors, and news pieces shaming others, the more numb we become to the human lives behind these stories, says Monica Lewinsky. The more numb we become, the more we click. It is a vicious cycle.

"All the while, someone is making money off of the back of someone else's suffering," Lewinsky adds. "With every click, we make a choice. The more we saturate our culture with public shaming, the more accepted it is, the more we will see behavior like [shaming], trolling . . . and online harassment."[8]

While it is true that wrongs should not go unpunished, you still need to question whether or not public shaming is the right way to address bad behavior. In other words, you need to think about whether initiating or participating in public shaming is really a good option or not, says Tauriq Moosa, a public shaming and free speech expert.[9]

"None of this means outrage is bad," Moosa says. "It just means unchecked outrage—comprised only of scorn—which so often results from publicly shaming, is unhelpful, if not a hindrance. There are better ways to respond than knee-jerk anger, even if

Often it can seem like there is an online mob poised and ready to condemn our beliefs and actions. Think seriously about whether you want to participate in this sort of behavior.

The Internet and social media are powerful tools. You have a choice as to how you want to use them. While it may seem fun to take people to task, it is much better to be a positive force in society.

Handling Pressures to Shame Others

Everyone is influenced in some way by the people around him or her. In fact, peer pressure can be both positive and negative. For example, positive peer pressure can influence you to make wise choices, while negative peer pressure can lead you down the wrong path.

What's more, when it comes to shaming others within the school community, kids often think that if they do not join in, they could become the next target. Not surprisingly, learning how to deal with this type of negative peer pressure is an important life skill, especially if you are experiencing pressures to shame others online. Here are a few tips for dealing with peer pressure in a healthy way.

Know who you are. Be sure you know who you are and what you want out of life. If you are sure about your values, you will be less likely to compromise them for someone else. It is easier to avoid pressures to publicly shame others if it goes against your beliefs. Additionally, if you already know who you are, you do not need to rely on publicly shaming another person to feel good about yourself or to feel like you belong.

Trust your gut. Make sure you know how to listen to your instincts. Remember, if something feels wrong, it probably is. Most of the time, publicly shaming another person will not feel like the right thing to do. Trust those feelings.

Make sure someone has your back. Everyone fares better with a good friend or a solid group of friends. Good friends never steer friends in the wrong direction. Additionally, they are more likely to have your back should you make a mistake online. They also are the least likely to sell you out if you are publicly shamed.

Learn how to say no. Being accepted by others is a good thing, but the need for approval should never motivate you to compromise your principles and publicly shame another person. Be sure you know how to say no to others and establish boundaries. If you master these skills, it will be much easier to say no or refuse to participate in public shaming.

Consider the consequences. Every choice you make comes with consequences of some sort. Remember that engaging in risky behaviors, such as sexting, can hurt you and others. They also open you up to public shaming. Before you engage in one of these behaviors, be sure you understand the risks involved.

Learn how to predict negative outcomes. If you are able to recognize the risks associated with making bad choices or following along with the crowd, you will save yourself a lot of heartache down the road. Be sure you know how to look at a situation and examine the possible outcomes. If it seems too risky, it is probably not a good idea to go along with the group.

the other person is wrong."[10] According to Moosa, there are two characteristics to public shaming that make it an issue. First, public shaming is basically mob justice; second, there is no regulation or middle ground when it comes to public shaming. When it comes to mob justice, Moosa says it is not justice at all because those who are doing the shaming have voices that overpower the accused. "If you think you have moral immunity in how you respond to an act you deem wrong," he says, "[and] if you're bolstered by witnessing mutual reaction and views from others *to* the wrong act, this is essentially *mob* justice."[11]

Sometimes the people doing the public shaming communicate even worse messages than the person being targeted, he says. For instance, they respond with expletives, name-calling, and threats. But the hypocrisy is not noticed, says Moosa, "because we are morally right and so can do no wrong."[12]

What's more, public shamers do not report to or answer to anyone. They get to be the accusers, as well as the judges, juries, and executioners, he says. "There is no one 'above' the group [and] the idea of defense is unknown."[13]

"So the next time you see a tweet that smacks of public shaming, think twice about retweeting it and joining the [shamers]," says Hansen. "If you are in a position to challenge the shaming, and have the courage to push back against the tide, consider being a hero in defense of a lonely victim."[14]

Ask yourself: Does this person's mistake really deserve public shaming on such a large scale? Do I really need to pile on with the others and expose his or her misstep to the world? What philosopher Friedrich Nietzsche had to say more than a century ago still applies today: "Be careful when you fight the monsters, lest you become one."

Chapter Notes

Chapter 1: Public Shaming Then and Now

1. Monica Lewinsky, "The Price of Shame," March 2015, <http://www.ted.com/talks/monica_lewinsky_the_price_of_shame/transcript?language=en> (accessed June 2015).
2. Ibid.
3. Ibid.
4. Ibid.
5. Ibid.
6. Lindsey Hoffman, "Public Shaming on the Internet," *Huffington Post*, March 3, 2015, <http://www.huffingtonpost.com/lindsay-hoffman/public-shaming-on-the-internet_b_6849036.html> (accessed June 2015).
7. Ibid.
8. Todd Leopold, "The Price of Public Shaming in the Internet Age," CNN, April 16, 2015, <http://www.cnn.com/2015/04/16/living/feat-public-shaming-ronson/index.html> (accessed June 2015).
9. Bonnie Tsui, "Friends with Benefits: Inside Facebook's Compassion Research Day," *Pacific Standard Magazine*, March 18, 2014, <http://www.psmag.com/nature-and-technology/friends-benefits-facebook-sociologists-social-media-74781> (accessed June 2015).
10. Ibid.
11. Sherri Gordon, "5 Things to Teach Your Kids About Digital Etiquette," Bullying on About.com, April 30, 2014, <http://bullying.about.com/od/Cyberbullying/a/5-Things-To-Teach-Your-Kids-About-Digital-Etiquette.htm> (accessed June 2015).

12. Jolie Lee, "#WhyIStayed: Powerful Stories of Domestic Violence," *USA Today*, September 10, 2014, <http://www.usatoday.com/story/news/nation-now/2014/09/10/why-i-stayed-hashtag-twitter-ray-rice/15385027/> (accessed June 2015).
13. Ibid.
14. Leopold.
15. Alexis Kleinman, "Social Media Makes Us All Bullies, Say Monica Lewinsky and Jon Ronson," *Huffington Post Tech*, March 31, 2015, <http://www.huffingtonpost.com/2015/03/31/public-shaming-jon-ronson_n_6978816.html> (accessed June 2015).
16. Lewinsky.
17. Stephen Marche, "The Epidemic of Facelessness," *New York Times*, February 14, 2015, <http://www.nytimes.com/2015/02/15/opinion/sunday/the-epidemic-of-facelessness.html?_r=0> (accessed June 2015).

Chapter 2: An Inside Look at Public Shaming

1. Interview with author, (July 2105).
2. Ibid.
3. Ibid.
4. Ibid.
5. Ibid.
6. Ibid.
7. Malini Goyal, "With FB & Twitter, Public Shaming Gets a Makeover; But Roasting on Social Media Can Have Dramatic Impact, " *The Economic Times*, April 5, 2015, <http://economictimes.indiatimes.com/articleshow/46808131.cms?utm_source=contentofinterest&utm_medium?=text&utm_campaign=cppst> (accessed June 2015).

8. Jeanna Bryner, "Schadenfreude Explained: Why We Secretly Smile When Others Fail," *Live Science*, December 9, 2011, <http://www.livescience.com/17398-schadenfreude-affirmation.html> (accessed July 2015).
9. Ibid.
10. Ibid.
11. Anne Collier, "From Public Shaming to Public Compassion," *Net Family News*, February 17, 2015, <http://www.netfamilynews?.org/public-shaming-public-compassion> (accessed June 2015).
12. Lisa Firestone, "Is Social Media to Blame for the Rise in Narcissism?" *PsychLive*, 2015, <http://www.psychalive.org/is-social-media-to-blame-for-the-rise-in-narcissism/> (accessed July 2015).
13. Collier.
14. Christine Roberts, "Slut-Shaming Trend Sweeping Internet, Adds Meme Form to Adolescent Cyberbullying," *New York Daily News*, January 7, 2013, <http://www.nydailynews.com/?news/national/adolescents-memes-cyber-bully-article-1.1235246> (accessed June 2015).

Chapter 3: Shame Comes at a Cost

1. Amanda Todd, "Amanda Todd's Story (Original Video by Her)," YouTube, October 2012, <https://www.youtube.com/watch?v=v2QRbl3H0ug> (accessed June 2015).
2. Krissy Darch, "Why Isn't Anyone Talking About the Misogyny Involved in Amanda Todd's Life and Death?" *Vancouver Observer*, October 12, 2012, <http://www.vancouverobserver.com/blogs/feminista/why-isnt-anyone-talking-about-misogyny-involved-amanda-todds-life-and-death?page=0,1> (accessed June 2015).
3. Todd.

4. Anne Collier, "From Public Shaming to Public Compassion," *Net Family News*, February 17, 2015, <http://www.netfamilynews.org/public-shaming-public-compassion> (accessed June 2015).
5. Cole Stryker, "The Problem with Public Shaming," *The Nation*, April 24, 2013, <http://www.thenation.com/article/problem-public-shaming/> (accessed June 2015).
6. Melissa Kirk, "Shame on You! Do You Use Shame to Control Others?" *Psychology Today*, June 26, 2011, <https://www.psychologytoday.com/blog/test-case/201106/shame-you-do-you-use-shame-control-others> (accessed June 2015).
7. Ibid.
8. Ibid.
9. Walter Torres and Raymond Bergner, "Humiliation: Its Nature and Consequences," *Journal of the American Academy of Psychiatry and the Law Online*, June 2010, <http://www.researchgate.net/publication/44668302_Humiliation_Its_Nature_and_Consequences> (accessed October 2015).
10. Collier.
11. Nina Burleigh, "Sexting, Shame and Suicide," *Rolling Stone*, September 17, 2013, <http://www.rollingstone.com/culture/news/sexting-shame-and-suicide-20130917> (accessed June 2015).
12. Ibid.
13. Luke Gilkerson, "Two Teen Rape Victims Shamed to Death," Covenant Eyes, April 16, 2013, <http://www.covenanteyes.com/2013/04/16/rehtaeh-parsons-audrie-pott-suicide/> (accessed June 2015).
14. Burleigh.
15. Jon Ronson, *So You've Been Publicly Shamed* (New York: Riverhead Books, March 2015), p. 247–49.

16. Sherri Gordon, "How to Spot Suicide Warning Signs in a Bullied Friend," Bullying on About.com, August 2, 2014, <http://bullying.about.com/od/Victims/fl/How-to-Spot-Suicide-Warning-Signs-in-a-Bullied-Friend.htm> (accessed June 2015).
17. Ronson.
18. Ibid.

Chapter 4: Inside the Minds of Public Shamers

1. Sam Biddle, "And Now a Funny Joke from IAC's PR Boss," *ValleyWag*, December 20, 2013, <http://valleywag.gawker.com/and-now-a-funny-holiday-joke-from-iacs-pr-boss-1487284969> (accessed June 2015).
2. Sam Biddle, "Justine Sacco Is Good at Her Job, and How I Came to Peace with Her," *Gawker*, December 20, 2014, <http://gawker.com/justine-sacco-is-good-at-her-job-and-how-i-came-to-pea-1653022326> (accessed June 2015).
3. Jon Ronson, "How One Stupid Tweet Blew Up Justine Sacco's Life," *The New York Times Magazine*, February 12, 2015, <http://www.nytimes.com/2015/02/15/magazine/how-one-stupid-tweet-ruined-justine-saccos-life.html?_r=0> (accessed June 2015).
4 Biddle, "Justine Saaco Is Good at Her Job, and How I Came to Peace with Her."
5. Ibid.
6. Ibid.
7. Ibid.
8. Ibid.
9. Ibid.
10. Ronson, "How One Stupid Tweet Blew Up Justine Sacco's Life."
11. Ibid.

12. Ibid.
13. Todd Wasserman, "Social Media-Based Public Shaming Has Gotten Out of Control," *Mashable*, March 24, 2013, <http://mashable.com/2013/03/24/public-shaming-out-of-control/> (accessed June 2015).
14. Nick Bilton, "When the Cyberbully Is You," *New York Times*, April 29, 2015, <http://www.nytimes.com/2015/04/30/style/when-the-cyberbully-is-you.html?smid=tw-share&_r=2> (accessed June 2015).
15. Ibid.
16. Wency Leung, "Why Do Some People Take Delight in Online Shaming?" *The Globe and Mail*, April 9, 2015, <http://www.theglobeandmail.com/life/relationships/why-do-some-people-take-delight-in-online-shaming/article23861243/?cmpid=rss1> (accessed June 2015).
17. Ibid.
18. Ibid.
19. Ibid.
20. Ibid.

Chapter 5: Keeping Shaming at Bay

1. Neetzan Zimmerman, "Should This Woman Have Her Life Ruined Because She Posted a Stupid Photo on Her Own Facebook Page?" *Gawker*, November 20, 2012, <http://gawker.com/5962189/should-this-woman-have-her-life-ruined-because-she-posted-a-stupid-photo-on-her-own-facebook-page> (accessed June 2015).
2. Steve Annear, "Lindsey Stone: Woman Fired From Job After Posting Offensive Photo to Facebook Page," *BostInno*, November 21, 2012, <http://bostinno.streetwise.co/2012/11/21/lindsey-stone-fired-for-facebook-photo/> (accessed June 2015).

3. Rheana Murray, "Company Praised for Firing Woman Who Took Disrespectful Photo Next to Soldier's Grave," *New York Daily News*, November 22, 2012, <http://www.nydailynews.com/news/national/praise-stone-fired-facebook-pic-article-1.1206392> (accessed June 2015).
4. Jon Ronson, "'Overnight Everything I Loved Was Gone,' The Internet Shaming of Lindsey Stone," *The Guardian*, February 21, 2015, <http://www.theguardian.com/technology/2015/feb/21/internet-shaming-lindsey-stone-jon-ronson> (accessed June 2015).
5. Ibid.
6. Sherri Gordon, "5 Reminders for Teens About Selfies and Cyberbullying," Bullying on About.com, May 30, 2014, <http://bullying.about.com/od/Cyberbullying/fl/5-Reminders-for-Teens-About-Selfies-and-Cyberbullying.htm> (accessed July 2015).
7. Sam Biddle, "Justine Sacco Is Good at Her Job, and How I Came to Peace with Her," *Gawker*, December 20, 2014, <http://gawker.com/justine-sacco-is-good-at-her-job-and-how-i-came-to-pea-1653022326> (accessed June 2015).
8. Jenny Shank, "5 Tips for Avoiding Public Shaming and 3 Tips for Recovering," *Media Shift*, July 14, 2015, <http://mediashift.org/2015/07/5-tips-for-avoiding-a-public-shaming-and-3-tips-for-recovering/> (accessed August 2015).
9. Amanda Lenhart, "Teens, Smartphones and Texting," Pew Research Center, March 19, 2012, <http://www.pewinternet.org/2012/03/19/teens-smartphones-texting/> (accessed July 2015).

Chapter 6: What You Can Do If You Have Been Publicly Shamed

1. Anne Collier, "From Public Shaming to Public Compassion,"

Net Family News, February 17, 2015, <http://www.netfamilynews.org/public-shaming-public-compassion> (accessed June 2015).
2. Ibid.
3. Interview with author.
4. Ibid.
5. Ibid.
6. Ibid.
7. Ibid.
8. Ibid.
9. Ibid.
10. Ibid.
11. Ibid.
12. Ibid.
13. Ibid.
14. Ibid.
15. Ibid.
16. Jenny Shank, "5 Tips for Avoiding Public Shaming and 3 Tips for Recovering," *Media Shift*, July 14, 2015, <http://mediashift.org/2015/07/5-tips-for-avoiding-a-public-shaming-and-3-tips-for-recovering/> (accessed August 2015).

Chapter 7: How to End Shaming for Good

1. Brock Hansen, "Why YOU Should Know the Shocking Dangers of Public Shaming," *Your Tango*, 2015, <http://www.yourtango.com/experts/brock-hansen/what-can-be-done-about-public-shaming-expert> (accessed August 2015).
2. Ibid.
3. Ibid.
4. Ibid.
5. Mike Robbins, "How to Be Truly Empathetic," *Huffington Post*, December 18, 2011, <http://www.huffingtonpost.com/mike-

robbins/power-of-empathy-_b_1015610.html> (accessed August 2015).

6. Ibid.
7. Cole Stryker, "The Problem with Public Shaming," *The Nation*, April 24, 2013, <http://www.thenation.com/article/problem-public-shaming/> (accessed June 2015).
8. Monica Lewinsky, "The Price of Shame," March 2015, <http://www.ted.com/talks/monica_lewinsky_the_price_of_shame/transcript?language=en> (accessed June 2015).
9. Tauriq Moosa, "The Dangers of Public Shaming, Mob Justice and Scolding on the Internet," *The New Statesman*, January 2014, <http://www.newstatesman.com/voices/2014/01/dangers-public-shaming-mob-justice-and-scolding-internet> (accessed August 2015).
10. Ibid.
11. Ibid.
12. Ibid.
13. Ibid.
14. Hansen.

Glossary

adulterv—When someone has an intimate relationship with a married person.

body shaming—Making negative comments about someone else's body; the purpose of the statements is to make the person feel bad about or embarrassed of his or her body.

branding—A type of public shaming used years ago that involves burning an identifying mark into a person's skin with the purpose of labeling him or her.

bullying—Words or actions intended to harm another person who is weaker or has less power; usually occurs more than once.

bystander—Someone who witnesses public shaming, bullying, or cyberbullying.

context—Circumstances that provide a setting or background for an event, idea, or comment.

context collapse—Term used by researchers to describe the lack of context found on social media.

cyberbullying—Bullying that occurs online or through digital media.

digital etiquette—A set of expectations or manners when using the Internet or digital media.

domestic violence—Also known as intimate partner abuse or domestic abuse; abuse that takes place between married or dating partners.

emotional intelligence—Sometimes referred to as a person's

EQ; it is the ability to understand another person's emotions and handle interpersonal relationships with skill and ease.

empathy—The ability to understand and share the feelings of another person.

everyday sadist—A person who enjoys inflicting pain on others but is not a criminal, nor do they have a mental illness.

flogging—A type of public shaming used years ago that involved beating someone with a whip or stick.

hashtag—A word or phrase preceded by a pound sign (#) that is used on social media to identify posts and messages that relate to a specific topic.

LCSW—Licensed clinical social worker.

mob justice—When authority is given to a multitude; it is usually not regulated or controlled.

narcissism—Excessive interest in oneself or one's appearance, often at the expense of others.

networking—A method used to develop professional relationships.

pillory—A device used years ago to publicly shame people; it consisted of a wooden frame with holes in which the head and hands can be locked.

public shaming—Humiliating another person online.

schadenfreude—Occurs when people get pleasure from the misfortune of others.

selfie—A photo that someone takes of himself or herself, usually using a smartphone, that is posted online.

slut shaming—Attacking women and teen girls for the way they look and dress, as well as their perceived level of sexual activity.

social media—Websites that allow people to connect with other people to share information and photos.

stockades—Upright wooden posts or stakes used years ago in public shaming.

suicide—The action of killing oneself intentionally.

trolling—Deliberately and sometimes secretively making people angry on the Internet.

For More Information

National Center for Victims of Crime
2000 M Street NW, Suite 480
Washington, DC 20036
(202) 467-8700
www.victimsofcrime.org

National Crime Prevention Council
1201 Connecticut Avenue, NW, Suite 200
Washington, DC 20036
(202) 466-6272
www.ncpc.org

Pew Research Center
1615 L Street, NW, Suite 700
Washington, DC 20036
(202) 419-4300
www.pewresearch.org

Further Reading

Gordon, Sherri Mabry. *Are You Being Abused?* New York: Enslow Publishers Inc., 2015.

Morin, Amy. *13 Things Mentally Strong People Don't Do*. New York: William Morrow, 2014.

Ryan, Peter. *Online Bullying (Teen Mental Health)*. New York: Rosen Pub Group, 2011.

Tanenbaum, Leora. *I Am Not a Slut: Slut-Shaming in the Age of the Internet*. New York: Harper Perennial, 2015.

Taylor, Julia V. *The Body Image Workbook for Teens: Activities to Help Girls Develop a Healthy Body Image in an Image-Obsessed World.* Oakland, CA: Instant Help, 2014.

Websites

Bullying Information
bullying.about.com

Common Sense Media
commonsensemedia.org

Connect Safely
connectsafely.org

Cyberbullying Research Center
cyberbullying.us

Monica Lewinsky—The Price of Shame TED Talk (video)
ted.com/talks/monica_lewinsky_the_price_of_shame

Pew Research Center (Internet, Science, and Tech)
pewinternet.org

Safe Kids
safekids.com

Stop Bullying
stopbullying.gov

Index

Q

R

S